# On the
# CAMINO
# REAL

# On the CAMINO REAL

## A Westward Quest Series Novel

## Stephen L. Turner

SUNSTONE PRESS

SANTA FE

Sunstone books may be purchased for educational, business, or sales
promotional use. For information please write: Special Markets Department,
Sunstone Press, P.O. Box 2321, Santa Fe, New Mexico 87504-2321.

Book design » Vicki Ahl
Body typeface » Book Antiqua
Printed on acid free paper

---

Library of Congress Cataloging-in-Publication Data

Turner, Stephen L., 1957-
  On the Camino Real : a western quest series novel / by Stephen L. Turner.
    p. cm. -- (The westward quest series ; 2)
  ISBN 978-0-86534-728-1 (pbk. : alk. paper)
  1. Scots-Irish--United States--Fiction.  I. Title.
  PS3620.U76596O5 2009
  813'.6--dc22

                              2009026463

---

Published in

WWW.SUNSTONEPRESS.COM
SUNSTONE PRESS / POST OFFICE BOX 2321 / SANTA FE, NM 87504-2321 /USA
(505) 988-4418 / ORDERS ONLY (800) 243-5644 / FAX (505) 988-1025

# Preface

THIS WORK OF HISTORICAL
fiction is the second in the Westward Quest Series.
The first book, *Out of the Wilderness*, follows the arrival
of Thomas Turner from Ireland to South Carolina in
1749. He carved a plantation and home from the raw
frontier wilderness and defended it against Indians
and British soldiers.

*On the Camino Real* follows his grandson, Aaron
Turner, as he hears the call of the West and sets out
to explore and settle in Texas in the days when it was
still part of Spain.

Only a few historical glimpses remain of Aaron
in deeds and wills and a few other documents. He
inherited 59 acres near the family plantation in South
Carolina which he later sold to finance his travels
west. We know he was married to a Cynthia Simmons
in Georgia who was a widow with children from a
previous marriage. Aaron had one or more children
with her before the marriage ended, it is assumed, by

her death. The children did not live with Aaron, including his own son Aaron, Junior. On his death bed he leaves a token inheritance to these step-children and Aaron, Junior. He married a widow, Nancy King, who had children from a previous marriage named Lucius, Marcus and Louisa. He and Nancy had other children in Georgia and Texas. The actual date of their arrival in Texas is unknown. However, the location of their land is established. They lived on the Camino Real as it passed through what would later become Leon County near the Navasota River. A small cemetery near there holds the remains of some grandchildren and very likely Aaron Turner. Nancy remarried, but the marriage failed and she lived with her children for many years.

Aaron and his family would know the terror of the Texas Revolution and the infamous "Runaway Scrape," as the only land route out of Texas to flee pursuing Mexican troops was literally by their front door. They also saw the depredations of Indians, especially the dreaded Comanche. The fear of the "Comanche Moon" is quite real. The raid on Fort Parker by Peta Nocona was only a few miles from their home.

Aaron was ordained as a Methodist minister at some point before reaching Texas. His 1851 obituary survives to give a small glimpse of his life. Three of his sons, David, Noah, and Aaron Lloyd, enlisted in the Confederate army just a few miles from home in 1862. David was never to return. He is buried near Camp Douglas, a Union prison camp outside Chicago.

I have attempted to complete the missing parts of the tapestry of his long and interesting life with plausible fiction based on period research. The next book in the series, *Under Troubled Skies*, will continue Aaron's saga and adventure in Texas.

—Stephen L. Turner
2009

# Acknowledgments

THANKS ARE DUE TO several people. First is my wife, Roberta, for her patience with my limited computer skills and her encouragement. Next, my cousin, Ella Turner Bullard, freely shared from her treasure trove of family facts and history, as well as proof reading. My parents, Aaron Lynn and Alene Turner encouraged me to continue and provided proof reading and editorial advice. Thanks to the friends and family of mine who did not mind having their persona borrowed to model several of the characters. It is so much easier to write when you have a person in mind to know how they look and act and react in various situations. Finally, my gratitude is due to my editor and publisher, James Clois Smith, Jr., of Sunstone Press for his guidance, confidence and encouragement in my entry into the world of published literature. I would not have come this far without his expertise.

Stephen F. Austin, "The Father of Texas."
Etching by William Howard c. 1833.

General Antonio Lopez de Santa Anna.
Courtesy Library of Congress.

# 1

Fall 1814, at sea, off north coast of Cuba

THE LAST OF THE tropical night grudgingly gave way to the hazy gray of the pre-dawn morning. The sea was gently buffeting the bow of our trading brig *Liberty* as she shouldered her way slowly northwestward. Our companion, the three-masted trading ship *Ghost of Savannah*, under Captain Marion's command, sailed 200 yards to our lee. The gentle breeze was steady from the southeast, and the northern coast of Cuba was just visible as a purple smudge to our south.

The mainmast lookout yelled down an alarm. "Strange sail to windward!"

Captain Johnson on the quarter deck of *Liberty* barked, "Where away?"

"Dead south, sir. Topsails up, on a course to forereach us!"

Captain Johnson smiled. "The wolf has seen the sheep, Mr. Turner."

I returned his smile and wondered how I ever came to be here. I was named Aaron Turner after my father's brother. My grandfather, Thomas Turner, had come from Belfast to settle in South Carolina in 1749. My father, Thomas, Junior, was born there. They had fought side-by-side in the War for Independence.

I had inherited a small productive tobacco farm near my family's land in Marlboro County. My cousin in Savannah had convinced me to work in the shipping and trade business. I was twenty-one, six feet tall, with red hair and blue eyes hinting at my Scots Irish heritage. I had been appointed cargo master of both these vessels, answerable to Turner Shipping and Trade for the profitable disposition of freight. Our route took us to Havana, Vera Cruz, New Orleans, and back to Savannah. I was fluent in Spanish and French.

The lookout interrupted my thoughts. "She's hull up and closing fast, sir. Looks to be a corvette of about twenty guns. No commissioning pennant, either, sir."

Captain Johnson called to the first mate, Mr. Dulaney. "That means our wolf is a privateer. Set more sail, but be clumsy about it. We need to look like a panicked rabbit with a broken leg."

"Aye, aye, sir."

"Fire a leeward swivel gun to alert Captain Marion. He knows the plan."

The sides of both our ships had been painted flat black with a mixture of boiled linseed oil, turpentine and soot, as had the masts and spars. It made them almost invisible in the dark. The heavy canvas sails had been colored a medium gray to make them hard to see against the horizon both night and day. Both appeared to be only lightly armed trading vessels. That which was not seen was what made them deadly.

The upper four feet of the bulwarks had been covered with heavy canvas painted to look like the hull, then carefully tacked into place. This concealed the gun ports on both ships. *Liberty* had eight hidden gun ports on each side, and *Savannah* had ten. Each gun port carried a thirty-two pound carronade. Carronades were short, light-weight, fast-handling guns that threw enormous shells a short distance. Beyond one hundred yards, they were inaccurate, but at close range, the thirty-two pound solid iron shot could turn the oak sides of an enemy ship into matchwood. When fired with dozens of one pound grape shot, they cut the rigging into pieces, splintered spars and masts, and killed several men in a single blast. The deadliest to human flesh was canister, thirty-two pounds of musket balls which could spew a path of lethal destruction at close range. One broadside of canister from those monsters could turn a deck into a slaughter house.

As the two "lambs" played their part of panicked inept escape, the "wolf" moved in for the kill. The corvette was sleek and fast, painted black with a red stripe along her sides. Obviously well-built, she was rigged with good rope and canvas. The mouths of nine cannon thrust from her starboard side as she turned to run parallel to our course. The cannon appeared to be nine pounders, known for their accuracy. The privateer fired a shot across our bow and hoisted a British ensign.

"Mr. Dulaney, hoist the Spanish flag."

Perhaps this ruse would buy a few moments to lure them closer. The corvette put her helm to starboard, closing the range to fifty yards. They fired another shot, just feet in front of the bow. They hailed us to drop sail and let them board to check our papers. Playing my part in the plan, I shouted, "Lo ciento, capitan. No se!" (I am sorry, captain. I do not understand.)

Now within twenty yards, their captain barked in Spanish to drop sail or he would fire.

"Si! Yo comprende!" (Yes, I understand!) At this cue, some of the crew fumbled with the clew lines to the foresail. At the same time, the canvas cover was ripped away as we hoisted the American flag, and the guns were run out.

Captain Johnson bellowed, "Fire!" All eight carronades belched solid shot from point blank range into the corvette. All the swivel guns fired at the captain and the helmsmen on the quarterdeck. Clouds of smoke wreathed our deck as the guns spewed out death and destruction.

Following our broadside by only seconds, four guns answered from the corvette. As the breeze cleared the smoke, we could see five of her nine gun ports were nothing but gaping holes. I shuddered as the shots from her nine pounders thumped solidly into our port side. The fast-handling carronades had been reloaded. Their second volley destroyed the last of the enemy's starboard guns. Her mainmast was sagging forward under the pressure of the remaining sails. She tried to port her wounded helm away from our guns, but the corvette responded sluggishly.

Captain Johnson grabbed a speaking trumpet and shouted to the blood covered deck of the corvette, "Strike your colors now!"

As the damaged ship gradually turned away from us, her name was readable on the transom. She was the *Mary G.* of Kingston. She fired a single stern gun, sending a nine pound ball whistling across our deck, smashing our long boat in the waist into splinters. The single shot killed one of our men and injured two others.

The carronades had been loaded with grapeshot. They fired in unison into the vulnerable transom. The blast of 196 one pound iron shot tore through the wood of her stern, destroying her steering, and wrecking havoc on her gun deck.

She drifted aimlessly toward us. There was no rudder or anyone left alive on the bridge to steer or give orders. A bloodied sailor appeared at the wreckage of her stern, cutting the flag halyard. The British ensign fluttered slowly into the sea behind the helpless ship. The fight was over. Our men broke into a loud chorus of cheers.

A group of eleven men appeared on her deck holding a white flag. She slowly drifted toward us. We quickly took in our sails, as we dropped fenders over the side to cushion the expected collision.

Once she was along side, we lashed her to our port side, went aboard to take our prisoners and assess the damage to our prize. Our consort took up position to windward to watch for other ships attracted by the cannon fire.

There were eleven men with only minor wounds, but six below deck were too badly injured to survive. The rest of the crew was dead, as were all the officers. It had been bloody work. Our surgeon tended to our wounded, then crossed over to minister to the wounded prisoners. For those below, there was no hope. By the time the prisoners on deck had been treated, the others had died.

The dead from both ships were sewn into canvas hammocks with a cannon ball at their feet. Captain Johnson read over the dead sailors, as one after the other was tilted into their watery grave. The "lambs" had slain the "wolf."

The eleven prisoners were given the option of being

released in one of the ship's boats with water and provisions to sail back to Jamaica, or signing on the ship's books to work until we reached Vera Cruz. After brief discussion, all of them elected to stay. They were left aboard our prize to help with repairs. We transferred enough additional men into her to keep her former tenants from mischief.

The corvette's mainmast needed immediate attention. It had received a blow from one of the thirty-two pound shot, leaving a crater the size of a pumpkin in the three foot thick mast. Tension from the rigging was causing the mast to bend forward. The maintop mast was removed and lowered to the deck, and the rigging was removed. The wounded mast was reinforced by lashing thick six foot long oak stays over the damaged area and the rigging replaced.

All three ships set sail for Vera Cruz, and the remainder of the damage was repaired during the voyage. Our prize would bring a fat price there.

---

Our mission was to call upon the commandant of the Vera Cruz garrison. He commanded the San Juan de Ulua fortress guarding the harbor and all its defenses; not a barrel of sugar moved from the docks without his consent. Even the captains of Spanish warships answered to the tall handsome aristocrat Lieutenant Colonel Antonio Lopez de Santa Anna.

In 1810, while Spain was preoccupied with Napoleon, a movement for the independence of Mexico erupted in the sleepy countryside, led by a priest named Father Hidalgo. A rag-tag band of peasants and merchants had raised arms against the

Spanish Royal garrisons and gained a foothold in the remote parts of Mexico. Spain had been able to stabilize the situation, controlling all the major cities and ports. But the revolutionaries hung on in the backcountry. Spanish troops patrolled the main roads, but there were places they dared not travel.

The revolutionaries possessed a few small privateers based in the ports of Yucatan. They raided merchant ships then disappeared in the small harbors that dotted the coast. There were few Spanish warships to protect trade and chase the raiders. Although my sympathies lay with liberty from tyranny, my business was with the Royalists for now. Perhaps Santa Anna needed a small warship.

———————

After an appropriate wait to show his disdain, we were led into Santa Anna's beautifully furnished office. He stood, nodding to me; we had done business in the past. I introduced the two captains. He motioned for us to be seated, and a young lieutenant took our cloaks and hats. Smiling confidently, he took his seat behind a huge desk. The lieutenant brought each of us cool glasses of sangria, handing his commander an ornate goblet of gold.

"To your health, gentlemen." he said in perfect English.

"And to yours, Excellency."

"How may the government of His Royal Highness, the King of Spain, Mexico and the Indies be of assistance to you?"

I was amused at his effort to intimidate us with the title of the Spanish king, but dared not show it. "We have come to Vera Cruz to trade."

"But you have rarely asked to see me. My clerk handles merchant affairs. Perhaps there is something more important, maybe the corvette you have brought into my harbor?"

As usual, nothing had escaped his attention. I smiled. "Your Excellency attends to his duties well."

He turned to his aide. "Lieutenant Avila, have the gentlemen present their papers. If they are pirates, we must hang them."

The captains beside me shifted nervously in their seats, but we had come prepared. "Here are the papers from the ship which attacked us. You will see that she carried letters of marquee. Here are our papers for both our ships. My country has also granted us the same letters of marquee."

The lieutenant scanned the papers, placing them in the colonel's outstretched hand. Santa Anna perused the documents and returned them to his aide. "So you have taken her as a legal prize of war. What is this to me?"

"We had hoped your government might be willing to buy her into your service if you find her worthy of flying the flag of Spain."

He folded his hands under his chin. "Have her tied at the wharf tomorrow at nine. I will send someone to inspect her."

Just before 10 o'clock a handsome black carriage pulled by four magnificent matched black horses fitted with silver inlaid black harness rolled to a stop on the cobblestone wharf. A squadron of twenty lancers in full dress uniform escorted the carriage. A footman unfolded the step. Santa Anna appeared in an elegant and dashing uniform befitting a king, accompanied by Lieutenant Avila, a clerk, and a naval officer. I walked to the carriage, removing my hat. With a quick nod of acknowledgement, Santa Anna followed me to the ship. Every aspect of the ship and her armament was inspected.

"I believe she will serve our needs. I will offer you seven thousand ounces of silver for her and all her guns, fittings and stores."

I was not in a position to dicker with someone of his stature. I knew she would bring more elsewhere, but we were here and could not afford to offend our host. "Your Excellency is a shrewd businessman. I accept your generous offer. I also have something in appreciation of your personal attention to this matter." I offered a small leather bag filled with a handful of gold coins which I spread in my palm. Returning them to the bag, I extended it to him.

Taking it into his hand, he quietly slipped the pouch into his pocket. "For such a young man, you are wise in the ways of the world."

Our business concluded, we set sail for New Orleans. We were a little worse for the wear, but with a considerable profit for our troubles. Fate had smiled on us.

---

A steady south wind carried us to the approaches of the Mississippi River. We cautiously entered the mouth of the river which was famous for its treacherous shoals. Drawing less water, Liberty took the lead with a trusted man at the helm and another in the bow continuously casting the depth line. It was slow going, but the wind held favorable and we reached New Orleans on the evening of December 5, 1814.

With the ships safely tied to the wharf at Turner Shipping and Trade, we headed to the offices of the company agent, Charles Contois. There was some mail for us, but the main talk in the office was of the war. The British appeared to be preparing to launch an attack on New Orleans.

Charles told us what he knew. "Sir Alexander Cochrane's fleet has sailed from Jamaica with a combined force of ten thousand men. The general view is that he will not risk our batteries guarding the approaches to New Orleans or the shoals of the Mississippi. If a ship were to strike a sand bar, it would be a sitting duck. For now, we wait to see where they will attempt a landing."

"It sounds like we have time for a run up to Natchitoches to finish our trading."

"Aye, the steamer *Samuel Brown*, under the command of my nephew, Robert Contois, stands ready to take on freight now."

"I hope this nephew of yours knows his business. The Red River is not a place for beginners."

"He is young, but he was raised on the rivers of Louisiana. I think he is half alligator."

The *Samuel Brown* was a tidy small stern wheel steamer. She had shortened stacks for navigating under over-hanging trees. Robert Contois was about my age, six feet tall with dark hair and a crooked smile. He was very outgoing and impossible not to like.

"So, Aaron, how do you like my little steam boat? Her draft is so shallow if the river drops we can break open a keg of beer and float another mile on the foam."

"Ha! If you can pilot her as well as you can talk, we should be fine."

---

We made our way steadily up the muddy waters of the Mississippi to the confluence of the Red River. Captain Rob had men at the bow continuously casting the lead line, as he cautiously felt his way across the shoals, sand bars, and snags of tangled timber that made this one of the most dangerous places on the river. There was no joking or boasting now as he eased the helm one way or the other, guided by ripples on the surface and the readings of the bow lines. Perspiration beaded on his face with the intense concentration.

Once we were safely into the Red River channel, he looked over his shoulder with a relieved smile. "See along that side how it looks like easier going than here? It is only a foot deep. A duck could run aground there. But here, against this bank, the channel is deep and clear, except for the branches hanging from the live oak trees."

"Why doesn't someone cut them back out of the way?"

"They ain't my trees. Are they yours? I'll drop you off while you go to work. We'll pick you up on the way back down if the gators don't get ya."

---

Finally, around a bend in the river, Natchitoches came into view on the west bank. Rob turned the steamer bow first into the landing, casting anchors fore and aft to keep the boat from drifting in the current. It was a bustling frontier town. The streets were unpaved and rutted with red mud. There was a road following the west bank of the river to the north and south, where it intersected the east-west road that connected Natchez on the Mississippi with Nacogdoches down in Texas. This was the Camino Real, or King's Highway, which continued to San Antonio de Bexar deep in Texas and on to Mexico City. To the east, the road led to Natchez on the Mississippi. It didn't look very royal. Louisiana had been ceded from Spain to France, only to be sold to the United States. The Camino Real didn't become property of the King of Spain until it crossed the Sabine River into Texas.

The town of rough log cabins and sawn lumber stores fanned out along the intersection. The streets were filled with oxen straining before wagons, pack mule trains led by swearing muleskinners, and horses of every description. For all its rough edges, Natchitoches pulsed with life and vitality.

Our trade goods were carried by sweating slaves to the establishment of our friend Louis bon Chance. He was a successful trader, known from New Orleans to St. Louis and deep into the wilds of Texas. That night at supper, Louis spoke glowingly of the unspoiled beauty and promising wealth of Texas and its forests and prairies. The image he painted touched something deep within my soul. The very mention of Texas set my skin tingling and my imagination running. I did not know it then, but he had planted a seed deep in my heart that would one day grow into the stuff of dreams and destiny that would forever change my life.

# 2

December 1814, New Orleans, Louisiana

WITH CAPTAIN ROB AT the helm of *Samuel Brown* guiding us down the river, we were soon in New Orleans. The city was alive with tension we could feel even before we docked.

Rob soon had the answers to our questions. "Well, Aaron, I don't like it a bit. Cochrane unloaded his Redcoats on the Gulf coast at Pea Island east of the Mississippi with a bunch of flat bottom shallow-draft boats. They say each one can carry a platoon of men and has a small cannon mounted in the bow. They crossed the Pontchatrain; all we had to stop 'em were five little gunboats. The Brits sunk all of them, and landed sixteen hundred men ten miles south of here on this side of the river. There ain't a corporal's guard along the whole river road to stop 'em."

"Is there a plan to do anything?"

"Yep, Andy Jackson has come down the Mississippi in flat boats with two thousand men and more on the way."

"What do you think my chances are to get my two ships down to the Gulf?"

"Mister, you are already trapped. You're here until this mess is settled."

The mood was gloomy at our offices and warehouses. Charles Contois was waiting for me. "Aaron, I'm glad you are here. Things are bad, really bad. If the British take New Orleans, they'll loot and burn our warehouses and everything in them. They are asking for volunteers to help stop them. We have already volunteered to do what we can. Do you think the men on your ships would join us?"

"They're all free men, but I think they will fight. I'll talk to my captains."

Counting the men from both ships and the warehouse, we had 160 combatants. As ranking representative of Turner Shipping and Trade, I was chosen as commander. I had no experience with war on land. At least I knew the men I would lead. Hopefully, someone would tell me what to do with them.

I found General Andrew Jackson, "Old Hickory," in an upstairs office in the Cabildo near St. Louis Cathedral. Tall, lank, with piercing eyes like an eagle, he stood as I entered. "Well, what do you want, boy? I have a battle to fight!"

"My name is Turner, sir. I am in command of one hundred and sixty volunteers. We came to fight in your battle, but maybe you don't need this 'boy's' help."

"Lord bless ye, but ain't you a feisty one. We need everyone who can tote a gun. How are your men fixed for arms?"

"We're armed to the teeth with rifles, cutlasses, plenty of

powder and shot, and eight nine pound cannon we can remove from our ships." There was no need to mention the carronades. They were mounted on sliding wooden carriages and would have been nearly impossible to move without wheels.

His blue eyes brightened. "I'll assign you to Colonel Rodriguez' Fourth Regiment. Since you are commanding better than two companies, you'll be Major Turner until this thing is over. Get those cannon down to the Chalmette Plantation today, Major."

I could hear my mother's voice ringing in my mind. "Aaron Turner, what have you gotten yourself into now?"

―――――――

At Chalmette Plantation, we found every man, both slave and free, who could use a pick and shovel digging a deep ditch and piling all the dirt on to the north bank of the ditch. The ditch and embankment ran from the river across the river road all the way across the cane fields into the cypress swamps east of the river. Redoubts were built to mount the variety of guns, including the eight we brought. The redoubts were reinforced with tightly packed bales of cotton and logs. The guns were set to sweep the entire approaches to the defensive line. A forward redoubt protected the corner of the line where it met the river. On the west bank of the Mississippi, the warship *Louisiana* was grounded and armed with two twenty-four pounders and two twelve pounders to provide an effective crossfire. A modest contingent of infantry was positioned there to slow any British advance on the west bank and to protect the *Louisiana*.

On December 23, Jackson sent a battalion to attack the

British before they could be reinforced, but it was driven off by stiff resistance. By the next day, massive reinforcements arrived bringing the Redcoat's strength to 8,000 men, under the command of General Edmund Packenham. He tried to find a way to flank the Chalmette defenses, but the roads were almost impassable. Local militias and common citizens harassed them with deadly accuracy from the cover of the swamps where the soldiers could not follow.

Jackson received welcome reinforcements swelling the American defenders to over 5,000 plus a group of Cherokee and Chickasaw Indians. Our native allies were gifted fighters from cover. They were assigned to protect our left flank near the swamp.

On Christmas Day, Packenham led a reconnaissance in force against the earthworks. It was cold and overcast with a light drizzle falling. While the British artillery provided cover, his infantry approached our defenses to probe our strengths and weaknesses. Our cannon returned fire, aiming for their guns.

The shrill whistle of the shells over our heads was unnerving. The impact was like Thor's hammer pounding into the soft dirt. Captain Rob had brought another twenty men from his steamer to reinforce us. "Lord, Major, this is some sorry way to celebrate Christmas."

"Aye, I'd rather be sitting at home eating roast beef by a warm fire. It's getting noisy around here."

An eerie silence settled across the mist-covered fields as the guns ceased firing, followed by the shrill voice of fifes and the rattle of drums. A double rank of red uniforms with white cross-belts appeared through the fog only one hundred yards away. Jackson's order to hold our fire was strictly observed. At fifty yards, the order raced the length of the line: "Fire!"

Our rifled muskets not only outnumbered the British line, but were much more accurate than their smooth-bore Brown Bess muskets. Their front rank fired and fell back, the second line doing the same. Then their field officer ordered a full retreat. The commanding officers had been counting our rifles and distribution along the line. It was hard for me to comprehend sacrificing men's lives to discover this information. Later, a mounted officer rode into the field under a flag of truce. He requested permission to retrieve their dead and wounded. His request granted, stretcher bearers carried their bloodied comrades from the field.

On December 28, Packenham began a series of probing attacks to further explore our defenses. They were easily repelled, but we knew we had seen only the tip of the iceberg. The nights passed cold and damp in the tent city behind our soggy earthworks. Jackson had set up his headquarters in the plantation house at the west end of the line. On New Year's Eve, he called an officers' meeting. "Gentlemen, my scouts tell me the enemy has used the recent attacks as a diversion to move heavy artillery within reach of our lines. Tell your men to keep their heads down. We will have an unpleasant New Year."

I suspected what was to come was worse than what we had seen so far. My hands were shaking as I unbuttoned my jacket in my tent. I called Charles, Rob, and our two sea captains to join me. "Well my friends, it seems our uninvited guests plan to start the New Year off with a bang. They have moved heavy guns to their line. Tell the men to stand strong tomorrow. I have a gift for each platoon of men." I gave them several jugs of whiskey to divide among the men.

New Year's Day, 1815, started with the roar of the British heavy guns. Captain Rob climbed to the top of the embankment and bowed with a flourish of his hat. "For what we are about to receive, we are truly thankful." He turned and dropped his trousers exposing his bare buttocks to the Redcoats. As his men laughed, a twenty-four pound shot slammed into the embankment only feet from him, knocking him head over heels unhurt into our lines. "Boys, I think they mean business!"

My command stayed huddled close to the earthworks. The soldiers in the redoubts carefully laid their guns aiming for the British artillery. Unfortunately, they were doing the same thing to us. By noon, our forces had lost three guns. At this rate, we would be in bad shape soon. But by two o'clock their guns fell silent. Their quartermaster had failed to send enough powder and shot to the line. Our supplies were plentiful, so we continued to blaze away at them as they retreated. Fate had provided us a respite.

For the next week, both camps stared at each other out of range. The British had been careful to deploy their men behind low walls of logs, with skirmishers all around. There would be no surprise attacks this time. Our scouts reported that many wagon loads of powder and supplies had been unloaded at the enemy camp. The wait for the main assault would not be long.

The American line had not been idle, strengthening our redoubts and the great earthen wall. A company of cavalry had taken up position in our rear to drive back any serious breach of our line. Continuing rain had turned the fields in our front into a furrowed muddy morass.

In the pre-dawn darkness we heard assembly bugles in the British camp. A heavy dripping fog hung over us. Sound seemed to carry unnaturally far in the fog. As the fog lifted, the muddy field was filled with Redcoats, their bayonets glittering in stray rays of sunlight. They slogged forward through the mud, finding it difficult to maintain formation. Our remaining cannon opened fire with round shot, tearing bloody holes in the tightly packed enemy ranks. The holes were filled with more men from the rear, and still they marched on toward us. The *Louisiana* opened up a cross-fire from the west shore with her four large guns. The ranks became more ragged, but still they pressed relentlessly forward. As they drew closer, we changed to grape shot sending hundreds of one pound balls of iron ripping through their lines. When they were within one hundred yards we changed to canister shot, each gun spraying a lethal blast of musket balls like enormous shotguns. The Redcoats fell like ripe fruit in a high wind. Our riflemen appeared at the top of the earthworks to add deadly rifle fire into the advancing enemy. Our Indian allies peppered their right flank with rifle and musket fire from the cover of the swamp. Finally, the front British rank knelt and fired, as the second rank passed them and repeated the process, continuing until all six ranks had fired and the first was now reloaded and firing again. They relentlessly pressed forward, oblivious to the carnage all around them; they were selling their lives dearly, for from our cover, our own casualties were light.

As they reached the flooded ditch, the front ranks tried to cross, but the ditch was too deep, and the banks too steep and slippery to climb back out. Those who entered the ditch did not come out. Their officers ordered ladders to the front to try to cross the ditch and mount the wall, but the ladders had been left behind in camp. As the mortal rain of rifle balls and canister poured into their men, they finally sounded recall. They retreated in an orderly fashion as we continued to kill them from the relative safety of our muddy parapet. As they continued to retreat out of rifle range, the cannon fired first grape shot then solid shells into their decimated troops having a grisly effect.

Following the repulse of the first wave, we heard musket fire across the river on the west bank. A detachment of 700 British had crossed the river before wading waist deep water to attack the men guarding the *Louisiana*. The defenders were overwhelmed by their numbers and the ship quickly fell to the invaders, but not before driving steel spikes deep into the touch holes of the cannon, rendering them useless.

In the early afternoon, the British were seen forming for a second attack. We repeated our defensive sequence as before with solid shot, followed by grape, then canister and rifle fire. There was no crossfire from across the river now. Enemy skirmishers were successful in driving our Indian allies back into the protection of the left end of the earthworks. It was chilling to watch the Redcoats falling in such great numbers only to press forward. This time, we could see scaling ladders in their midst. We directed our rifle fire to the men carrying the ladders and the officers. But as they dropped, others took their place.

When they reached the ditch fronting our parapet, it was choked with the floating bodies of their comrades. As soon as the ladders were settled into place, withering rifle fire cut the British to shreds. Our cannons continued to belch death and destruction with each charge of canister. Packenham himself took the field to urge his men forward only to be swept dead from the saddle by a blast of canister in full sight of his men. General John Lambert, the second in command, assessed the carnage where his brave men were being dashed to pieces against our defenses. He ordered a retreat, and we continued to hammer them as they left the field. The battle was over. The 8,000 British had suffered 2,037 casualties; our force of 5,000 had lost seventy-one.

After retrieving their dead and wounded, the British retreated down the river road, redeployed their boats and rejoined the fleet at Pea Island. On February 12, they took Biloxi, Mississippi. Before they could advance against Mobile, word arrived that the Treaty of Ghent had been signed ending the war. It had been signed on December 24, 1814. The greatest American victory of the war had been won after the war had ended.

# 3

## February 1815, Savannah, Georgia

*LIBERTY* AND *SAVANNAH* made the return trip to their home port uneventfully. There was a buoyant joy because of the American victory. Due to the turmoil following the end of the war, our trading voyages were delayed until things stabilized. Memories of the Battle of New Orleans were vividly burned into my mind. The sour smell of gun smoke and the sickening odor of blood and death lingered in my nostrils. The rattle of musket fire, the roar of the cannon, the screams and whimpers of the wounded haunted my thoughts. The sight of men vaporized into a red mist and the mangled bodies invaded my days and nights. It had been a horrible thing, yet I had played my part and rejoiced in our victory. The nausea and sudden shudders of cold chills gripped me unexpectedly. I needed to get back to South Carolina to discuss these things with my father.

I booked passage on a coastal trader for the easy sail to Georgetown. I spent the night with cousins there before heading up the Pee Dee early the next morning in a scow. A cold wind from the northeast filled the small lug sail, assisting the twenty-four slaves who toiled at their oars against the current. Late in the day, we were bumping into the dock at Cheraw Landing where I rented a good horse for the ride to Turner's Crossing. The familiarity of the countryside was a balm to my troubled mind. The wind gained strength and heavy snow began to fall. By the time I reached the bridge that marked the corner of our plantation, four inches of snow covered the ground. I unsaddled and groomed my horse in the huge log barn my grandfather had built and trudged through the snow to the cabin that had been my home.

As I pounded on the door, I could hear Father's voice. "I'm coming. Do ye think me deaf?" He opened the door with a look of irritation on his face, which was quickly replaced with recognition. "Aaron! You have been away so long. Rebekah, the prodigal has returned!"

Wiping her hands on her apron, Mother grabbed me tightly and showered my face with kisses and tears. "Aaron, I'm so glad you are here. It has been over a year since your last letter."

As we ate supper, the story of the capture of the privateer, the encounter with Santa Anna, and the Battle of New Orleans spilled out. Father gave me a knowing glance. "Son, with the snow cover, the hunting should be good tomorrow. Think you can keep up with an old man?" Reaching into the corner he retrieved a gun which he handed to me. "I want you to have this. It was your grandfather's double barreled Manton .45 rifle brought with him from Ireland. There isn't a finer gun in

America. I still have the one he gave me when I was a boy."

"Father, James is the eldest; he should have it."

"No, he will have mine soon enough."

The smell of coffee awakened me the next morning. Father and I were soon seated on a fallen log watching the green wheat that shone through the fresh snow. A fat doe stepped quietly into the early morning sunlight, followed by a huge buck. Father indicated the first shot was mine. It was only fifty yards away, an easy shot for the fine Manton. I eased the hammers back, carefully sighting on the majestic buck. I slowly shifted my aim and dropped the doe in her tracks. The buck bounded away into the woods.

Father smiled at me. "I have passed a shot at him twice myself. I'm glad you did, too." I returned his grin as I walked to retrieve the doe. As we sat on the log, field-dressing the deer, father asked, "So was your first taste of battle as sour as mine?"

"Aye, Father. I can't describe it. I was exhilarated at the time, regretful afterwards, and haunted by it in my dreams even now."

"Son, I still have nightmares of the battles I fought. Sometimes the chills and the nausea return. At the time, we had no choice but to fight; there was no other way. Freedom extracts a higher price than we know." We sat in silence staring across the field, each lost in deep thought. Finally, Father patted my shoulder. "Let's get home so Mother can fry us up some venison steaks." The brief talk with Father had helped me more than I could have imagined.

Over the next few days, I got to see most of my relatives around Turner Crossing. One morning I set out with my older brother, James, to see the fifty-nine acre farm I had inherited from

Grandfather Thomas Turner. It was a good productive farm with a solid cabin and out buildings. The tenant had bought some tracts adjoining it, and reminded me how much he would like to buy it.

As my time grew short, I said my good-byes. I told Mother and Father I would try to return soon, but the words rung hollow.

———

The company kept a set of simple apartments above the shipping office where I stayed while in Savannah. Through my cousin, I was introduced to a Methodist minister who invited us to join him for supper. He had a beautiful daughter named Cynthia. She was widowed and had children from her first marriage. Within a short time, I found myself drawn to Cynthia, and we were married soon after by her father. It was not a happy marriage, for her children never accepted me. When she was expecting our first child together, I hoped that would unite us as a family. Her father encouraged me to study for the ministry and loaned me books for my next sea voyage.

As we sailed on our next trading trip, I found time to read *The Life of Christ, Prophesies of the Old Testament Fulfilled in the New Testament, Combined with the writing of Matthew, Mark, Luke and John in one Volume.* It was a huge leather bound book that took the whole voyage to read. I had to admit I really enjoyed it and wanted to read more.

———

When we docked in Vera Cruz, I spotted the commander's

ornate carriage and his bodyguard of Spanish Lancers. He seemed to be involved in resolving some dispute. However, when he noticed me, he sent Lieutenant Avila to ask me to wait a moment. His business concluded, Santa Anna briskly walked up to greet me. "Mr. Turner, it is a great pleasure to see you, or perhaps I should say, Major Turner?" Seeing my surprise he smiled. "I have many sources."

"Your Excellency, it is an honor to see you. I was a major of volunteers at the Battle of New Orleans for a few weeks only. I have been Aaron Turner all my life."

"You are modest, Major. The corvette you sold His Majesty has proved most useful. However, there is something more you could do. Our supply of gunpowder and shot of all sizes from Spain is sometimes insufficient to our needs. If you believe you could be of assistance, Lieutenant Avila will provide the details."

After Lieutenant Avila carefully outlined their needs, we quickly set sail for New Orleans.

_____

As we neared New Orleans, we slowly sailed past the Chalmette battlefield. The ditch and embankment were still in place in case of further need, but the cotton bales and guns were gone. The battlefield where so many had died was sprouting new green growth of sugar cane. My throat tightened and my stomach rolled as memories came flooding back. I hoped I would never experience the horrors of war again.

Charles met us at the dock. On explaining our unusual request, he answered there was plenty of gunpowder to be had in

Kingston. There was a lead mine, the Mine a' Breton, in Missouri run by Moses Austin and his son, Stephen, that could supply all the lead we needed. He would have it ready for our return trip.

During the trip home, I finished *Commentary on Acts of the Apostles*, and completed exams over both books. Word soon reached our Savannah office that the gunpowder had arrived in Kingston. *Liberty* and *Savannah* would not be able to handle such a large order alone. There was a beamy three masted trader, *Agnes*, waiting for us in Kingston. When we arrived in Kingston, we found *Agnes* already in ballast with 24 pound cannon balls and iron bars. The powder hoy was alongside finishing her lading. The kegs were handled like delicate blown glass. One mistake could sink half the ships in the harbor. We exchanged our cargoes of lumber and rice for cannon balls and powder. The men aboard the powder hoy were exhausted by the time the last of the cargo was loaded.

We arrived at the mouth of the Mississippi without incident to pick up the lead. We were berthed on the west bank of the river to protect other shipping if something should go wrong. Flat boats gingerly maneuvered alongside to unload their cargo of .69 and .75 caliber lead shot and additional lead ingots. The *Agnes* looked way past her prime, but Captain Williamson assured us she was as solid as the day she was built.

I could not keep myself from teasing him. "And just when would that have been? In the reign of Good Queen Bess?"

"Why no, sir. Her hull was laid down in Seventeen and Sixty-one. She is only fifty-four years old."

We slowly worked our way southwest across the Gulf of Mexico to Vera Cruz. The third night out we could see sheet lightning in the distance to the southwest.

"Some poor sailors could be having a rough night of it there, Captain Johnson."

"Aye, it could be an early season hurricane blowing itself out. We'll miss the storm, but probably have some rough seas and rain."

By the next afternoon, a long rolling swell was moving to the northeast at cross-current to the normal sea. This caused a rough chopping motion that shook the ships right down to their keels. Soon, a heavy rain followed. We altered course to decrease the pounding the ships were taking from the cross-current and reduced sail. It was a long, hard night, as the jarring tested the strength of the ships. The cargo was checked constantly, as a loose barrel of powder could prove disastrous.

In the gray dawn the rain had lessened and the waves were more forgiving. Our ship was intact. Signal flags flashed out to the other two ships to report their condition. I used a telescope to inspect *Savannah*. I watched as she raised a flag indicating no damage. Crossing the quarterdeck, my heart sank as I saw the *Agnes*, even before her signal flags were raised; it was obvious she was in serious trouble. "Captain Johnson, what do you make of that?"

"She's hoggin'. See how her bow and stern don't rise together? She is sagging away from the middle like a sow's back. If she is emptied of her cargo, she might make it to Tampico if the weather holds. But I don't think that much cargo could be jettisoned in time to save her."

Captain Williamson had already begun to try to save his ship well before dawn. His crew frantically worked the cargo hoists to bring up crates of musket balls, lead ingots, and cannon balls, and drop them over the side. Her long boat put over the side. Her second mate and a double bank of oarsmen rowed hard for *Liberty*. As we watched the last of her heavier cargo go over the side, we could see that her damaged keel was getting some relief. She hogged less with each wave. They were starting to bring the kegs of powder on deck to load into boats for transfer into the other two ships. The old girl might make it yet.

*Agnes'* long boat hooked on to *Liberty's* side as her mate climbed aboard. "Sir, Second Mate McLain. Some of the barrels of gunpowder have broken open in the hold. He has wet the cargo deck down—" He was interrupted by a blinding orange flash followed instantly by an explosion that knocked us off our feet.

When we looked where the *Agnes* had been, a column of water was falling back into the sea. A wave caused by the blast spread in an ever widening circle, rocking *Liberty* hard enough to knock us from our feet. Debris of all sizes rained down from the sky. As the wind blew the smoke away, the sea was littered with pieces of the ship and pieces of bodies. Dead fish floated slowly to the surface. We only recovered seven bodies from the wreckage.

# 4

## February 1816,
## off the coast of Vera Cruz, Mexico

AFTER WORDS WERE spoken over the bodies, we set all sail for Mexico. We were all anxious for this voyage to end. Within a week, Vera Cruz was in sight. A familiar corvette sailed out to meet us proudly flying the Red and Gold flag of Ferdinand IV. We were to dock at the harbor fortress of San Juan de Ulua which guarded the approaches to the harbor. Lieutenant Avila greeted us at the fortress. It was obvious he had been promoted. His uniform was now that of a captain in the Royal Infantry. "Your cargo will be unloaded here in case of an accident. Did you not sail with three ships?"

"Yes, Captain, we did. One of them exploded with the loss of all hands."

"Madre de Dios! I am sorry." he said as he crossed himself.

Once our deadly cargo was unloaded, we rowed across to the office of our agent there. I made our report to the astonished clerk and asked of the local news.

"The commander had been made a full colonel over all the Royal forces along the Gulf from the Rio Bravo to the Straits of Cuba. His success in dealing with the coastal rebels earned his promotion. The captured corvette played no small part in his success. He gives our ships preferred berths and government contracts. The rebels are driven into hiding in the northern mountains and the southern wastelands. Ferdinand IV has returned to the throne and deposed that impostor, Joseph Bonaparte. Perhaps now we will enjoy peace and prosperity here in Mexico."

Mexico had known its share of prosperity but had never known peace for long.

Santa Anna's beautiful coach, escorted now by forty lancers and a heavily guarded mule drawn wagon, clattered to a stop on the wharf. The great man himself, accompanied by Captain Avila, emerged from the coach. He was resplendent in his new uniform of a full colonel. "Good morning, Major Turner. I understand you have delivered most of the munitions ordered, but at a great cost in lives. I am sorry to learn of your losses."

"Good morning, Excellency. It is unfortunate that we were not able to deliver the entire order."

"You have done me more service than you know, Major Turner. I will not forget it." He placed a silk pouch in my hand that contained a beautiful gold medallion deeply embossed with his own image. "I give these only to those who have done me special service as a reminder of gratitude for their loyalty."

On the return voyage to Savannah, I had to say I was truly glad this voyage was over. Domestic life was difficult for me. My frequent absences did not endear me to the children. I had grown up in a close knit family; this feeling of disunity was unsettling. I tried to talk to Cynthia about it without much progress. I gradually came to realize that we did not love each other. However, I resolved to make things better.

I had passed the exams for *Survey of the Old and New Testament.* I even learned some Greek, but no Hebrew. I read extensively from the writings of Calvin, Luther, and Wesley. Cynthia's father gave me copies of *The Common Book of Prayer* and *The Methodist Ministers' Companion.* In March of 1816, I passed both a written and oral ordination exam and was ordained as a Methodist minister.

The spring trading season was peaceful and prosperous. I enjoyed the familiar sights of Kingston, Havana, Vera Cruz and New Orleans. I made a quick run up the Red River to Natchitoches to trade and see Louis bon Chance.

"Aaron, the Spanish are actually encouraging settlers to come to Texas. They think this will protect them from the Indians. But not many are taking them up on the offer. It is still a pretty dangerous place. The Spaniards have pulled their garrisons back to Goliad and San Antonio, leaving but a small garrison in Nacogdoches. Maybe someday you will let me show you?"

At the mention of Texas my spine tingled. I could feel the tug of adventure pulling me there, but I knew for now, I could not. "As you say, Louis, someday."

I returned to Savannah in early September. I was anxious about Cynthia and the baby. The welcome from Cynthia and her parents was warm enough, but cold from the children. The baby's arrival was traumatic. The baby was turned the wrong way and the mid-wife had to summon the doctor. The baby, a boy, was born distressed and weak. Cynthia had lost a great deal of blood. She was too weak to nurse the baby, so we hired a Negro wet nurse. Our son was named Aaron, Junior. Over the next few weeks he grew steadily stronger, while Cynthia grew steadily weaker. By November, she seldom left the bed, and her mother had to bathe and clothe her. I felt useless and in the way. The baby did not attach to me, although I tried everything I knew. He would cry until his nurse took him from me. By December, Cynthia began to experience a cough and fever the doctor diagnosed as pneumonia. A week later, her frail body gave up. Her last request had been that her mother would raise little Aaron and the other children. The step-children blamed me for her death. After her funeral, I had a long talk with her parents and moved back to my small apartment on the waterfront. I experienced a strange sense of guilt as if our failed marriage and her death had been my fault. I felt a frustrating sadness that my only child would have nothing to do with me. But I was also conscious of an unexpected sense of relief, a release from an obligation, and a return of my freedom.

With the spring of 1817, I was ready to see Texas for myself. Being aboard *Liberty* again was a welcome change. After our routine stops, we finally arrived in New Orleans. Charles was waiting at the dock when we moored. "Well, Aaron, what's been keeping you?" he grinned. In response to my puzzled look, he continued, "I thought you could use some good company on your trip to Texas." He had already bought the trade goods for our trip. There were iron bars for blacksmiths, ingots of lead to be melted for shot, flasks of gunpowder, musket flints, and a few rifled muskets, plus hand tools, house wares, bolts of cloth, piloncillos of brown sugar, coffee, spices, and garden seeds. Things that could be damaged by water were wrapped in water-proof canvas with an outer layer of oiled leather. The smaller items were placed inside water-proof tins fitted into oiled canvas panniers. He had arranged for Louis bon Chance to have a good set of pack mules and more supplies waiting at Natchitoches.

The *Samuel Brown* was tied at the docks to take on our goods. "Ahoy, Major Turner, ahoy!"

"Hello, Captain Rob! It's good to see you. Is this bucket of bolts ready to take us to Natchitoches?"

"Aye, the *Samuel Brown* is always ready for a paying proposition. I've got a notion to go with you to keep you and Charles out of trouble. I've already got someone to run my routes for me while I'm gone."

Louis was waiting for us at the landing. "Welcome my friends! We have been expecting you. Marie has cooked a feast for you." True to his word, we had a fine supper of baked ham, sweet potatoes, corn bread and peach cobbler. "Aaron, I got you a fine set of mules, broke to ride and to pack, and a couple of good muleskinners, the Teel brothers. They're young, but they know what a mule is thinking before he does, and are crack shots, too. You'll like them. I also got you a guide. He knows the country, speaks several Indian languages, English, French, and Spanish plus, he is a good shot and cook, too."

"Who is it, Louis? Sounds like a man I can use."

A familiar voice came from down the table. "You already know me, Mr. Turner. I won't let you down." It was Louis' son, Chance. He smiled as I showed my surprise. He was sixteen, over six feet tall, with dark hair and blue eyes. He was dressed in buckskins and boots, with a huge knife stuck in his belt. Of course, Chance was an obvious choice. I would never regret taking him as our guide.

---

The next morning, I awoke to a circus of noise coming from the street. Through the window I could see two young men trying to keep twenty bay mules under control. They had managed to get tangled into a giant knot. The braying drowned out the shouts of the two muleskinners. Gradually they got one mule after another peeled away from the confusion and tied individually to the hitching posts fronting Louis' store. The older of the two was Nick Teel. He was eighteen, six feet tall and built like a bull. He carried a heavy braided leather bullwhip and an arm load of halters. Cody Teel was only thirteen, almost as tall as his brother, but with the slender build of a growing boy. I could tell at first sight that I was going to like them. They had riding saddles on six mules and pack saddles on the other fourteen. Louis had provided us with food and the other necessities of a long trip. Each man was to have two rifled muskets in scabbards and a pair of saddle pistols. These were huge .69 caliber pistols with 12 inch barrels. They could fire a single ball or a ball topped with a handful of buckshot. We all had good buckskins, heavy boots, and wide brimmed hats. Everyone was responsible for their own small clothes and some sturdy clothes for warmer weather. Cody had traded someone for a large smelly coon skin cap. It looked too hot for any kind of weather, but he was proud of it.

After a quick breakfast and hurried farewells, we got assembled in traveling order and set out on El Camino Real, the King's Highway. Chance took the point, scouting the road ahead for potential problems, followed some way back by me. The Teel boys came next, each leading seven mules. Rob and Charles brought up the rear. The road was heavily used near Natchitoches, but farther west, it was just a wagon track. The late afternoon sun reflected off water ahead, the Sabine River. We paused on the east bank as Chance rode across the ford to test the river bottom. The muddy water was stirrup deep and 150 feet wide, but it was a magical place. The wind in the cottonwood trees whispered secrets and the swirling water murmured mysteries. My heart raced and my skin tingled as the Sabine's water splashed on me while my mule trotted across the ford, baptizing me into the brotherhood of those who had come under the spell of Texas. The scenery looked identical on both banks, but this was Texas, the fabled land of promise, unseen dangers, strange peoples, and untapped resources. Here on the Camino Real our odyssey was just beginning.

# 5

Spring 1817, Camino Real, eastern Texas

NOT FAR FROM THE Sabine was a glade on the north side of the road. It was surrounded with mixed pine and hardwood forest near a small clear stream. It was obvious from the scars left by previous camp fires that we were not the first to stay here. Nick and Cody unsaddled the mules and covered the panniers with a heavy tarp weighted down with rocks. They hobbled the mules, watered them in the creek, and let them graze the lush grass in the meadow.

Chance was the camp cook. He opened an oiled leather pouch to reveal pinto beans he had been soaking all day. Dry wood was at hand and clean water from the creek. As the beans slowly began to bubble in the heavy cast iron pot, he sliced in some salt pork. A large pot of coffee was set to boil by the fire while he stirred up corn meal batter. When the coffee was done and the beans almost ready, he poured the batter into two greased Dutch ovens. The aroma had drawn us all around the cook fire. Finally, Chance announced, "Chows up!" Each one of us got a generous helping of beans, cornbread, jerky and fresh strong coffee. It was the kind of meal that could get a man on down the road.

The mules were left hobbled, tied to a heavy picket line and given a canvas feed bag of corn and oats. Two of us would be on guard the first half of the night, and another two the last half. Two would be allowed to sleep all night and we would rotate duty each night. I partnered with Chance on the second watch. The night air hung over us like damp velvet; the humidity increased as did the mosquitoes. Chance produced a leather pouch filled with a vile smelling concoction which he rubbed on all his exposed skin, and I did the same. "What is this awful stuff?"

"Rancid bacon grease, ground sassafras leaves and marigold flowers. Don't you like it?" he grinned.

"If it works, I guess I can stand it."

"It works good. Keeps the skeeters away and the flying monkeys, too."

"Flying monkeys?"

"Yep. You seen any around here?" We both laughed at his joke.

We heard raccoons in the trees near us. We didn't want them to spook the mules, so a few well aimed rocks sent them scurrying. We could hear a pack of coyotes celebrating life with their hunting song. I had always loved to listen to them. The plaintive call of a red wolf was answered first by one, then by a second wolf; I felt the hair on my arms and back of my neck stand up. They weren't likely under ordinary circumstances to bother a group like ours, but they had the potential to take down a mule or a man at any time. The mules shifted nervously, but a few calming words settled them.

Just before day break, I helped Chance get breakfast started. He mixed a stiff cornmeal dough with just a little lard and salt, then patted them into thin cakes which he cooked in a greased skillet until they had browned just a bit. He filled them up with mashed up beans left over from the night before and rolled them up. The aroma of the cooking and the coffee had drawn a crowd. We each had a couple with some hot coffee.

Cody asked, "Chance, this is pretty good. What is it?"

"Corn tortillas filled with beans. You better like it, 'cause that's lunch today." He handed each one of us three more and a little jerky in morrals of tightly woven grass. Nick and Cody got the mules saddled and loaded while the rest of us broke camp. Charles refilled all the canteens, and Rob helped water the mules. We were on the road by full daylight, eating as we rode and drinking from our canteen. As the weather was good and the road was dry, we only stopped to water the mules. We covered a lot of miles that day on the Camino Real. What an impressive name for such a pitiful trail. It was just barely fit for a wagon or a mule, much less a king! Chance had ridden ahead and returned with news of a Caddo village a few miles ahead. They had invited us to be their guests and to bring our trade goods.

———

The Caddo were friendly. Their word for friendly was *tejas* which usage had corrupted to *Texas*. Their village was remarkable. Their homes were arranged in an ordered fashion, each one shaped like an enormous beehive twenty to thirty feet tall. They had a framework of wood covered with thick thatch with a smoke hole at the top. The insides were lined with frames for sleeping compartments, two and three levels tall, screened with grass mats for privacy. Hides and furs were used for bedding. They also had large well-tended gardens with all sorts of vegetables and corn. They even grew a little spindly, poor quality tobacco.

That night they treated us to a feast of venison and vegetables. We shared some of our tobacco with them, which they seemed to enjoy. We spread out our trade goods on blankets. There was considerable interest in the steel knives, hatchets, axes and house wares. They needed powder and shot, too. We traded for fine pelts, softly tanned deer skins, dried venison and some nice blankets. One of their leaders, Man Who Laughs, wanted to trade for a rifled musket. We let him load it and try it. He motioned for two young men to bring out two fine native horses of about fourteen hands. They rode them for us, and it was obvious to see that the horses were of good quality. We accepted the trade, but sweetened the deal by adding three bags of shot and three horns of powder. The chief seemed to realize that he was being given a very favorable trade. He promised us that the Caddo people of his village would be our friends. As we left the next morning, we were given the hind quarters of a freshly killed deer and two morrals filled with fresh vegetables.

––––––––––

The road to Nacogdoches was crowded on both sides by dense pine woods and cane brakes. As we entered an especially narrow place, we had to ride single file. Seemingly from nowhere, a huge owl swept down on silent wings and cleanly jerked the coon skin cap off Cody's head. The owl came to rest in the top of a tree fifty yards up the trail clutching the cap. Cody was so mad that he pulled his rifle out of the scabbard and dropped the owl with one clean shot from the back of his mule. The unexpected shot set all the mules bucking and braying as they scattered into the cane brakes. Cody's mule ran under a low hanging limb and knocked him from the saddle. It was several minutes before order was restored, and much longer before we quit laughing. Cody walked to the dead owl, retrieved his cap, and replaced it on his head. We gave him the nick-name "Owl Killer" which stuck with him for many years.

--------

With the owner's permission, we made camp on a small farm a couple of miles outside of Nacogdoches. The Mexican farmer, Pedro Campos, showed us where we could pasture the mules and horses in a small fenced pasture with good grass and water. There was a three-sided log shed where we stored our trade goods and made our beds on the hay in the loft. We gave his wife, Juanita, the venison and vegetables which she made into a wonderful supper. We showed them our trade goods, but they had nothing to trade. For their hospitality we gave them a piloncillo of sugar, a bag of salt, some needles and thread and a good knife.

The next morning Charles and I rode into Nacogdoches. There was a two story fortified stone house where the alcalde had his office. We introduced ourselves and were given a cautious greeting. "What purpose do you gentlemen have for visiting Mexico?"

I answered in Spanish. "Your honor, there are six of us who have brought mules carrying goods to trade along the Camino Real all the way to San Antonio de Bexar. We have come to seek a letter of permission and to pay our import taxes."

"Yes, yes. I think that it can be done, but I am a busy man. It may take days or even weeks to complete the papers."

"I understand, Alcalde. I am prepared to offer a mordida because of the extra work we will cause you."

He smiled and reached into his desk. "Let me see. There are six men at eight reales each, and my men reported twenty mules at two reales each for a total of eighty-eight reales or eleven pesos."

I counted out the eleven pesos and gently placed two more on top. "Gracias, your honor."

He quickly wrote our names on a form, listing our mules and a general description of our wares. This was then embossed with a heavy official seal and his signature written prominently below. "You gentlemen will have no troubles if you present this document. I hope you have a safe and prosperous stay in Mexico."

———————

The next morning as we pressed farther west, the Camino Real showed evidence of heavier use. We met a train of huge two-wheeled carts pulled by lumbering oxen, goaded on by peasants on foot. They were protected by an escort of Spanish lancers under a lieutenant on a fine horse in a trail-worn, expensive uniform. The sergeant, corporal and all the men appeared to be mestizos. The light complexion and hair of their officer indicated he was of pure Spanish descent. He did not address us in person, but sent the sergeant to speak to us, as the lancers gathered in a loose circle around our party. The sergeant did not identify himself, but spoke politely. "The lieutenant would like to see your papers, if you please."

I dug into my saddles bags and produced the papers from a canvas envelope inside an oiled leather cover. I did not hand the papers to the sergeant. "I have registered with the alcalde of Nacogdoches and paid my fees. The papers are here, sealed by his own hand. Do you read, sergeant?" He shook his head that he did not. "Then I will give these to the lieutenant myself." I pushed my horse through the lancers to the arrogant young officer. He was indignant and raised his riding whip to strike me. I caused my horse to side-step to avoid the stinging blow. "Is this how the government of New Spain in the province of Texas treats lawful merchants traveling in peace on the King's highway? Tell me your name, lieutenant, so that I may speak to the governor in Bexar!" I rode my horse close enough to hand the papers to the angry, offended Spaniard. He scanned them, contemptuously handing them back.

"How do I know you are not bandits who have stolen these mules and these papers?" he demanded.

"How do I know you are not a peasant who has stolen a fine horse and uniform? Shall we return to the alcalde in Nacogdoches to decide this matter?"

The lieutenant flinched. "That will not be necessary."

"Tell me your name, Lieutenant."

A voice from the crowd of lancers called out, "His name is Don Luis Hernandez y Mendoza."

His eyes flashed in anger. "You are free to go. Give us no more trouble!"

"Thank you, Lieutenant Don Luis Hernandez y Mendoza. I will be sure to commend you to your captain." As the lancers parted for us to pass through; muffled laughter came from the men with the carts.

_____

The forest gradually changed to a predominance of hardwoods, sprinkled with pines. There were lush prairies frequently interspersed among the trees from small pastures of a dozen acres to huge open tracts of hundreds of acres. We made camp in one of these beautiful prairies. The hobbled livestock gorged themselves on the good green grass and watered from a small stream that trickled close to our camp. The grass grew belly deep on the horses and mules.

As Chance was getting supper started, a band of mounted Indians appeared in the edge of the forest 200 yards to the west. We all armed ourselves and stood ready for trouble. Cody and Nick quickly started catching the livestock and tied them to a picket line. Two well mounted Indians rode out to meet us, while the others stayed in the protective edge of the trees. I could see Chance visibly relax as he recognized them as Tonkawa. "They're peaceful and want to talk."

"Can you speak their language?"

"Can a skunk make stink? Sure I can. The Caddo, Tonkawa, the Wichita are all kin, and they all speak some kind of Wichita. That's why you brought me, Turner." His eyes glistened with humor. "They been huntin' and want to camp. Say they got a doe and a turkey to share. Their village is about two days from here. This 'uns name is Red Wolf, says he came huntin' to get away from his wife and kids."

I smiled at this, as I could sympathize with him. "Tell him this is why I came, too. He is welcome at our camp."

He seemed pleased, and motioned for the others to join him. He and his friend dismounted and walked into camp with us. They finished dressing their doe and set to roasting it over hot coals. They were delighted when Chance offered them a bag of salt which they rubbed over the roasting meat. They had fresh ears of corn, still in the shucks, which they placed around the edge of the coals to cook, turning them frequently. It was soon ready to eat and tasted delicious. We offered our guests coffee, but they did not care for its bitterness. Finally, the outer part of the venison was ready to eat. One of the Tonkawa carved off thin slices and passed them to each of us with a sparse sprinkling of salt. After we had been served, he fed his own men. The meat was tender and juicy. We all continued to eat until there was very little left but bones and gristle.

While our guests seemed friendly, we slept with our guns close at hand, surrounding our canvas covered mound of goods. Those on watch were especially vigilant, and none of us slept much. Red Wolf didn't have anything to trade, but asked us if we would meet him and his people on the banks of the Trinity River in four days. One of the main reasons for our trip was trade, so we agreed. We gave them a piloncillo of sugar and another pouch of salt. They gave us the turkey and promised to see us in four days.

We arrived at the Trinity in two days. We built a functional corral of post oak and pine. We also built a shelter with four posts set at the corners and a roof of tightly stretched well-tied heavy canvas. Post oak and pine logs were used to build side walls up about four feet high. It was just tall enough to provide cover to stand and fire. Our trade goods were stacked in the middle of our shelter. We felt relatively safe in our campsite. The mosquitoes were pretty bad, but Chance's evil smelling salve helped keep them away.

The next morning Chance and I decided to explore the road ahead. We found some faint wagon tracks turning north from the road. We followed the trail to a small cabin, corral and shed. We saw a man running from the field toward the house, and a shotgun appeared from a loop in the cabin wall. A woman's voice demanded, "State your business, or I'll shoot ya both!"

This was followed by an equally threatening male voice from the outside corner of the cabin accompanied with a rifle barrel. "What do you want?"

"We're just traveling through trading. We saw your tracks and smoke and thought we might find some white folks living here."

The female voice demanded "Well, here we are. Now, what do you want?"

"Look, miss. We ain't trying to cause you any trouble. If you don't want to be friendly, we'll just leave."

"What's your name, mister?" asked the man.

"My name is Aaron Turner; this here is my scout, Chance. You gonna put them guns down, or do you want the only white folks in a hundred miles to leave?"

"My name is Asa Smith, that's my woman, Janie. Sorry we're so unfriendly. There are plenty of bad folks wandering these parts. Y'all step down and water your horses and have some spring water and a bite to eat with us."

As we ate a meager lunch of left over cornbread and jerky, they told us their story. They had come from Arkansas and taken up eighty acres of prairie. They had about twenty acres under cultivation. He had shot some longhorn cows that had big heifers at their sides. They used the rawhide, ate and dried the meat, and kept the heifers to gentle down to start a herd. They had eight so far, and one nice young bull. Asa asked,"Y'all seen any signs of a preacher? I don't mean a bead mumbling priest, but a sure 'nough preacher. Me and Janie want to make our weddin' legal-like."

"Would a Methodist minister do?"

"Methody, Baptist, it don't matter much."

"I happen to be an ordained Methodist minister, and I'd be happy to do the honors."

Chance's mouth dropped opened, but he didn't say a word. I retrieved my Bible from my saddle bags, turning to a sample wedding ceremony in the back. I washed my hands and face, while the prospective bride and groom did the same. After a short ceremony, I produced a paper and pen on which I wrote the facts of the marriage, signed by all four of us, with Chance as a witness. Asa gave me a two-bit piece and asked us to stay on to supper. We declined as I wanted to see some of the country. We rode away west on the Camino Real. Finally Chance turned in the saddle, "Turner, I sure didn't figure you for no preacher."

"Am I that wicked?" I laughed.

"Naw, you just seem like common folk. Do I need to call

you reverend or something?"

"I guess not, as Protestants, and especially Protestant preachers, are not allowed in Mexico."

"I forgot we are all supposed to be good Catholics here!" he laughed.

———

Leaving the Smiths to God's protection we continued exploring westward along the Camino Real. At a turn in the road, I could see a thick stand of trees indicating a river or creek. We rode forward and Chance identified it as the Navasota River. On both sides of the Camino Real stretched the most beautiful prairie I had ever seen, interrupted by occasional oak mottes and a small creek away to the north. I felt my heart jump in my chest. This was it. This was my promised land. I knew at first sight that this was the place where I was meant to be. "Chance, this is it. This is where I want to settle."

"Major, there is still more of Texas to see."

"No. This is the place I see in my dreams at night. This is it!"

We rode to the river crossing. The banks were steeper here, deeper than the Trinity, making it less likely to flood. The land I had chosen continued to rise away from the river, so that it would not be flat and swampy like some of the crossings we had seen. The banks were not too steep, nor the river too deep for fording, and the bottom was rocky. Crossing over, we rode farther west, exploring as we traveled. Soon it was necessary to head back to our camp on the Trinity. Passing the place of my dreams once more, I knew that one day I would make it my own.

# 6

Spring 1817, Trinity River crossing,
Camino Real, eastern Texas

THE NEXT MORNING A
Tonkawa scout rode up to the river bank across
from our camp. He indicated the rest of their party
would be there by early afternoon, camping a ways
back east of the river. Chance told him we would be
expecting them. We hobbled the stock to graze while
we set up a display of our wares on blankets in the
shade. We only put out one of each item, as we didn't
want to reveal how much we had or risk getting all
of it stolen. Nick would return the livestock, still
hobbled, to the corral. Hobbled animals were hard
to steal. Cody was assigned to guard the covered pile
of goods. Chance would interpret as Rob and I made
trades, and Charles would keep the books.

Chance taught us a few words of Wichita.
"Major, you trust those Tonkawa?"

"Shoot, you know a lot more about this kind of
stuff than I do. What do you think?"

"These Wichita tribes, including the Tonkawa and Caddo, ain't too bad. They get along pretty good with white folks, except for a little stealin' once in a while. They hate the Comanche and Apache. I was thinking maybe we ought to keep our pistols on us, just in case of trouble. Cody and Nick can keep the rifles to cover us if we have to high tail it to cover."

Rob added, "I think Chance is right, and we don't need the whole dang tribe right up in our faces. They could steal us blind. We ought to let just a few come up at a time."

"Well, Captain Rob, it galls me to admit it, but you have a good idea."

We had just finished lunch when Red Wolf and the scout appeared across the river. He liked our trading proposal, and agreed that he would personally escort small groups across the river at a time. He left a handful of braves armed with muskets across the river, and he rode across with a group we assumed to be the tribal elders dressed in finery and mounted on good horses. The scout held their horses while they traded. The first items to go were two rifled muskets with powder and shot. After some discussion we settled on two horses for each rifle. With a whoop, the chief signaled a brave to lead across four horses. Rob took Nick's place at the corral so Nick could check out the horses. He looked at their eyes, teeth, feet and structure, before swinging up on each one to try it out. "They seem solid and healthy to me." That sealed the deal. He led the horses into the corral, while we gave them the two rifles, powder and shot. I loaded one for Red Wolf. He passed it to one of the oldest men. Taking careful aim, he drilled a small oak tree at seventy-five yards. They whooped their approval as the old shooter rubbed his boney shoulder and smiled a toothless grin.

The rest of the trading was pretty much ordinary. The Tonkawa wanted salt, sugar, an axe and shovel, and a little good tobacco. They paid us in good pelts and dried cow hides, some jerky and a morral of shelled dried corn. Chance did a brisk business of his own with a small supply of bright ribbons, glass beads, and small mirrors. Red Wolf invited us to eat with them. Sensing my hesitation, he said "We no steal from you tonight, if you no steal from us!" We laughed at the translation, and agreed to come over to eat two at a time.

I sent Chance and Nick first. They came back smiling and rubbing their stomachs. Rob and Charles went next and stayed longer. Charles explained, "Rob has got his mouth open talking so much, he is mighty slow to eat. He had those Tonkawa laughing and slapping their sides and they didn't understand a word he said!" Finally, Cody and I went to their camp. We were greeted by Red Wolf and the elders. There were several platters of various meats and vegetables, flat bread and honey. After we ate, the elder who had fired the rifle presented an ornate pipe filled with the tobacco they bought from us. Standing, he turned to each of the four corners of the winds, and blew a puff of smoke. He passed it to me. I repeated the ceremony and passed the pipe to Red Wolf who gravely saluted the winds and the earth. He in turn passed it to Cody. Realizing the gravity of the situation, he saluted the four winds, too, until a fit of coughing brought us all to laughing at his expense. Red Wolf had taught me a few more words of Wichita. He extended his hand in parting: "Friend." I replied: "Tejas." We had made a few more friends in Texas.

---

The Teel brothers built pack saddles out of wood and rawhide. We all now had good horses to ride, and we used the surplus mules to pack our newly acquired trade goods. We rested the stock the remainder of the day. They filled up on the good grass. Our hosts from the previous night had given us a large haunch of meat which had been slowly roasting all day over the coals. Chance boiled a big pot of vegetables to go with it. As the meat was ready, he sliced off tender, juicy pieces with just the right amount of salt. "Dang, Chance. This meat's good. What is it? Some kind of hog or bear meat?" Cody asked around a mouthful of roasted meat.

"No, the Mexicans call it 'carne de potrillo.' You like it?"

"Yep. Better than beef."

I looked at Chance and smiled. "Cody, it is horsemeat from a young colt."

He turned three shades of green, set his plate down, and finished chewing the bite in his mouth. Regaining his composure he said, "Heck, if I had known it was this good, I'd been eatin' 'em instead of ridin' 'em. Give me another slice, will ya?"

_____

After midnight, Rob and Charles had the watch. Something was making the livestock nervous. Charles had his back against a large tree. He leaned forward to wake us just as a huge arrow hissed through the air and sunk deeply into the tree, missing him only by inches. Blood-curdling screams shattered the night air, as shapes could be seen running from the forest to the cover of the live oaks across the road. The mules brayed in panic, and the horses nickered in alarm as eight huge naked warriors rushed from the darkness. They moved so quickly, and surprised us so completely, that we killed only one with our first volley. They were upon us before we could aim another shot, so the saddle pistols came into play. The buck and ball dropped three, but the other four were in our enclosure swinging massive war clubs. At point blank range, the .69 caliber balls topped with buckshot were deadly. We were able to fire our second pistols as the Indians lashed out with their war clubs. Having killed three of the four in the enclosure, the one surviving Indian ran from the enclosure straight for the river. Much to our surprise, three more previously unseen warriors appeared from behind us sprinting for the Trinity. Rob dropped one as he ran, but the remaining three could be seen desperately paddling a huge canoe with the current.

Stunned silence followed. "Y'all hurt?" I whispered. There was no response from the darkness. "Are y'all hurt?" I demanded. Finally, a murmur of assurance confirmed my companions were alive. The smell of the Karankawa was horrible. Their naked bodies glistened in the faint moonlight. The strong odor of rotted flesh hit me in the face like a hammer.

"Major, these are Karankawa. They live in small groups along the coast and raid up the rivers in canoes," Chance explained.

"But what is that smell?"

"They rub their bodies with rancid alligator fat to keep the mosquitoes away. Let me show you something." He picked up a fallen bow and an arrow. The bow was over six feet long, and the arrow was over three feet in length and bigger around than a man's thumb. "I seen a Karankawa shoot one clear through a bear at thirty yards." The dead Indians were each over six feet tall, and powerfully built, with elaborate tattoos. "They're cannibals. The Mexicans and the Indians live in dread of them. We were mighty lucky."

I felt goose bumps on my clammy skin: cannibals. And I wanted to settle on the next river, not thirty miles away. We gathered up our guns and began reloading, when Nick yelled at Cody, "Get up! We don't have time for you foolin' around!" He kicked him in the thigh, and watched in astonishment as Cody slumped over on to his right side, the left side of his hair matted with blood, running down his neck and back.

"Help me move him out by the fire so I can see what's wrong with him!" I yelled. By the firelight, we could see a deep gash in his scalp. I felt the bones of his skull, and didn't feel anything broken. Nick went back into the enclosure and found an arrow buried into the corner post head high where Cody had been standing. Apparently, it had hit him a glancing blow to the side of the head, knocking him out, then had buried into the post. I dug a bottle of whiskey out of my saddle bag and cleaned the wound. He didn't move or even groan. I cleaned a long horse hair and needle to sew up his cut. It wasn't pretty embroidery, but it ought to work. He remained mercifully unconscious as his wound was closed.

For another half hour Cody was still insensible. Nick cleaned him up and put him in his bedroll. Finally, rising up on one elbow, Cody murmured, "What happened?"

"Little brother, those Indians put your lights out. Now hush up, and get some sleep." Nick had spread his bedroll next to Cody where he could keep an eye on him.

None of us slept much that night. Chance had breakfast ready way before daylight. We were already on the road west just as the sky flushed violet in the east. By late afternoon we reached the Navasota. My heart raced as I saw the land I wanted so badly. However, we could not afford to get caught on the wrong side of the river if it rained, so we crossed over. Cody had a throbbing headache, but managed to keep up.

———

Once our camp was set and the stock grazing, I took my horse back across to explore my "promised land." I rode north to where a creek flowed into the river and followed it northeast until the prairie gave way to heavy forest. I followed the edge of the forest south until it intersected the Camino Real. I could already picture where our cabin and outbuildings would be located, and could imagine fields of corn growing in the summer heat. It was beautiful land with rich deep soil. The land seemed to possess a mystical hold on my soul. I knew this was the place I was meant to make my own. Perhaps it would own me more than I owned it. That night as I rested on my bed roll, I saw a falling star. I said nothing about it to my companions, but as I had done that night in New Orleans, I took it as a personal sign of destiny.

The next morning we found the land west of the Navasota pretty much the same, with rolling prairies and oak mottes. In an easy day's travel, we were on the banks of the Brazos de Dios, the Arms of God; but we just knew it as the Brazos. Chance tested the crossing. The muddy river was wide, deep in mid-stream with a strong current. The banks sloped down gently to the river. As the stock would have to swim most of the way, we insisted on tying Cody to his saddle. We made it safely across, and finding a good campsite not far from the river, we settled in for another night.

# 7

## Summer 1817, Brazos River crossing, Camino Real, central Texas

"NICK, YOUR BABY BROTHER seems almost normal this morning."

"Oh, yeah? How can you tell?" Nick laughed.

The Camino Real took a more southwesterly direction now as it headed toward San Antonio. The country was rolling prairie with many creeks lined with trees, and scattered islands of liveoak. Game, especially turkey and deer, was abundant. Seeing turkeys flying to roost late one afternoon, Nick shot one clean through the head at thirty yards. As we were hobbling the horses to graze, three Indians rode to within 200 yards of camp. We prepared for trouble, although they appeared friendly enough. Chance said they were Waco Indians and wanted to talk. With my approval, he waved them to come on into the camp.

"You boys be careful. We've had all the Indian trouble we can handle for a while." The Waco spoke Wichita also, so Chance could talk with them. The rest of us were picking up some of the language, too. They dismounted and presented us with a freshly killed turkey. Chance and one of the braves set about cleaning the birds. The leader of the three was a lesser chief known as Gray Feather. He had a large gray feather woven into his hair. He spoke enough Spanish that I could speak to him myself. I told him I was on a trading expedition to San Antonio. He was interested in our goods, so I showed him everything we had except the guns. There were several things that caught his interest, especially a bone-handled hunting knife. He had nothing to trade, but asked if his people could meet us where the Camino Real crossed the Colorado in a week. I agreed.

Chance cut the turkeys into frying pieces, rolled each piece in cornmeal and fried them in lard. He also whipped up a dried peach cobbler and a batch of biscuits. Supper was a huge success with our guests. Afterwards, I gave each of them a small pouch of tobacco and another of salt. To Gray Feather, I gave the knife he admired.

They told us of buffalo hunting to the northwest, and bear hunting to the east. They warned us of the Karankawa. I showed them the bow and quiver of arrows. Gray Feather said "Them eat mens. Bad Indians!" He told us of their dreaded enemies, the Apache, in the southwest and the even worse Comanche to the northwest. "Comanche" was the Wichita word for "people who love to fight." He warned us that the Comanche were even more cunning than the Apache and even fiercer fighters than the Karankawa. They kept the Spanish soldiers hiding in their forts at San Antonio and Goliad.

I thought to myself "What could be worse than the Karankawa?" One day, I would learn the answer to that question.

In a few days we reached the Colorado River. The land gradually became a little rougher the farther southwest we traveled. There was more prairie and fewer trees, except along the creeks and draws. Cedars replaced pines here. The grass was not so lush, but it looked like excellent cattle country, with some areas suitable for farming. We saw more wild cattle and horses here. A man could make a living gathering and selling unclaimed livestock.

We crossed the Colorado and set about building shelter for a few days. Cedar trees provided upright posts, and cottonwoods made the corral rails and the sides of our tiny "fort." The roof was a tightly stretched canvas tarp fixed to shed water. The "fort" shared a common side on the east with the corral.

The livestock were day herded with hobbles under the careful watch of Nick and Cody. Wearing hobbles, they would be almost impossible to stampede. We fed them dried corn from our morrals to supplement their grazing. We had pushed them hard the last few days. The country was open enough that one of us kept watch from the top of a small hill near our camp. Dust would give us advance warning in the daylight; our danger would come at night. We were camped where the territories of the Apache and Comanche overlapped. They generally avoided each other in this area, and the various Wichita tribes kept them in check to the east. The Spanish and Mexicans did not show their faces here without military escorts.

Gray Feather and his people arrived as expected, making camp across the river. We traded some rifles for good horses. We swapped some of our other trade goods for pelts, hides, jerky and dried corn.

We did not feast together with Gray Feather's people as we had with other tribes, as we all sensed a vague feeling of danger. The west wind whispered to us of danger in the air. Gray Feather and six other warriors offered to ride with us threes days down the Camino Real. At that point, we might expect to meet military patrols from San Antonio. We gladly accepted their offer.

On the third day west of the Colorado one of the Waco scouts came galloping in from the north. A war band of Comanche had spotted our party and headed our way. Here the Camino Real paralleled a wooded creek. We quickly moved the mules into cover along the creek, pulling off their pack saddles. We hobbled all the horses and mules, tying them to strong picket lines. The seven Waco stayed mounted and moved out to our right, hidden in the trees. We each had our two rifles, one of mine being the double barreled Manton, and our two saddle pistols. We unpacked the rest of our trade rifles, loaded them and divided them among us. Mules were highly prized by the Comanche for their eating qualities. And our twenty mules were loaded with trade goods. They must have presented a tempting target.

The war band was about twenty warriors to our thirteen, counting the hidden Waco. They were pretty tough odds, but we probably had superiority in number and quality of weapons. However, these were Comanche, the fiercest light cavalry in the world. My stomach tightened, and my mouth went dry. They appeared at the crest of a low rise about one hundred yards away, their horses prancing. They waved their war clubs, bows, and muskets, and jeered at us in an unknown tongue I took to be Comanche.

"Boys, listen close. Pick a man, and draw a close bead. On my signal, let 'em have it. Make it count! When I fire, the rest of you take your shot. Don't rush it."

"Ready. Fire!" At one hundred yards, the rifled muskets were much more accurate than the smoothbore guns the Indians had encountered from the Spanish soldiers. Six braves fell dead or wounded. The remainder flew into a wild, head-long charge straight into our position. We grabbed our second rifles, and fired a hurried volley at seventy-five yards, dropping three more. The others were now in bow range, firing from their charging horses. We were forced to seek cover, and only able to fire quick shots, killing two more. The rest descended on us like the hounds of hell at the edge of the edge of the trees. Timing their arrival perfectly, Gray Feather and his six braves took them in the flank. As they did, we emerged from cover with our deadly short range saddle pistols. The seven remaining Comanche were taken by surprise. They wheeled their horses for the ridge behind them. The Waco gave pursuit as far as the ridge, but let the others escape. A straight seven on seven fight against Comanche would be tough, even for our brave allies.

When they returned, we assessed the situation. No one was hurt, and we still had all the livestock. I realized if it had not been for Gray Feather, we would have likely all been dead. We ate a cold lunch of jerky and parched corn there in the trees. My hands shook so that it was difficult to hold my food. We repacked the mules, tightened the horses' cinches, and watered everything in the creek before heading out toward San Antonio. Before we left,

I presented Gray Feather with the best of the excess horses and a rifled musket. Gray Feather had held up his end of the bargain to escort us half way to San Antonio. He and his braves claimed the scalps of the fallen Comanche and then quickly left to return to his vulnerable villagers. The Comanche were on the warpath and he was away from his people. It was only then that I realized how much he had sacrificed to help us. I would not forget his bravery or friendship.

At dusk, we pulled into a grove of live oak trees to make camp. I felt more like a rabbit seeking a hole than a conquering hero. We did not take a chance on a fire, eating what cold food we had, and giving the stock grain to eat. None of us slept that night. Every quail or coyote call could be a Comanche in the darkness.

At dawn, we scurried down the road to the first stream where we could water the thirsty stock. Pushing the livestock to their limits, we encountered a large body of Spanish lancers under Lieutenant Rodriquez. I quickly produced our papers and paid special courtesy to the lieutenant. I needed help more than pride. He said there had been reports of gunfire, so he had been sent to investigate. He offered to escort us the rest of the way to San Antonio, about a day and a half's travel. I graciously accepted. We didn't stop until evening. He led us to a modest adobe home with adobe outbuildings and corrals. We put the stock in the corrals, rubbed them down, and fed them. The adobe corral had six foot tall walls with rifle ports built into the walls every four feet manned by the ranch's vaqueros. The adobe house was also equipped with rifle ports. The tile roof was fronted with a parapet of adobe sheltering even more heavily armed vaqueros.

Lieutenant Rodriquez introduced me to the owner of the hacienda, Don Fernando de Zavala. He explained that his vaqueros on his eastern range had heard shots and ridden for help. "I hope you will feel safe here as my guests." While the cooks were preparing supper, he had several bathtubs filled with hot water, and made soap and towels available along with clean cotton shirts and pants. When we had finished bathing, a barber appeared for haircuts and shaves. I felt like a new man, and sure did smell better!

Our supper was unlike any I had eaten in Vera Cruz. It was wonderful, spicy, rich and filling. The first course was a large bowl of posole. It is a sort of Mexican stew made with hominy, meat and chilies. This was followed by enchiladas, rice and beans, and sliced cucumbers on the side.

After supper, our host presented us with fine cigars and brandy. Cody wisely declined the cigar after his last experience with tobacco. We were given real beds to sleep in with cotton sheets and clean wool blankets.

Before leaving the next morning, I presented Don Fernando with the best rifle we had plus three pouches of powder and shot. There were also gifts for the cooks and the barber. Lieutenant Rodriquez and the lancers took up their positions, and we followed them southwest down the Camino Real.

# Summer 1817, San Antonio de Bexar, Texas

OUR ARRIVAL IN SAN Antonio de Bexar was disappointing. I am not sure what I was expecting, perhaps one of the Seven Cities of Cibola, layered in pure gold. I honestly had expected something more like Vera Cruz, with its fine Spanish architecture and landscaping. Instead, a town of dusty streets and adobe buildings stood shimmering in the late summer heat. The outskirts were filled with jacales, simple huts of brush and mud. There were prosperous irrigated farms and run-down missions along the river, but beyond the life-giving waters of the San Antonio River was parched, sparse grassland and thorny brush. There were some buildings that made an attempt at grandeur in a neglected sort of way. I had expected a pot of gold at the end of the rainbow, but had found a dusty bucket of rust.

Lieutenant Rodriquez introduced me to the

military commander. He looked disinterestedly at my papers and waived me out of his office. This would not be a choice post for an aspiring Spanish officer. I was directed to the alcalde, who was somewhat more pleasant in his greeting. "What brings you to Bexar, Mr. Turner?"

"I've come to explore the opportunities for trade in Texas, your Excellency. It is a country with vast potential."

"Do you think so? I find it rather dreary and dry, with too many Indians. The Apache and Comanche strike without fear, and the soldiers hide within their forts."

I thought it best to change the subject. "Actually, I have brought trade goods, horses and mules. Do you think there will be a local market for my goods?"

"You know that a permit is required to sell here?"

"Yes, your Excellency. I had expected as much."

"I will have my clerk prepare you a permit for only one peso, but it may take several days. If you would like one today, it is five pesos." I handed him five silver coins and he quickly issued a vendor's permit.

"We found an inn near the plaza with attached pens for our livestock. The inn wasn't much. Rob groused, "I've seen better pig pens back in Louisiana." The ticking on the corn shuck stuffed mattresses was stained to the point of greasiness with signs of bed bugs. A column of ants busily crawled up one adobe wall, while cockroaches scurried across the floor. We pulled the mattresses off onto the floor and placed our bedrolls on the rawhide straps of the bed frames.

The next morning we spread our wares in the shade of the tile roofed porch of the inn. It seemed the local residents needed everything we had. These had to be cash sales, as we didn't plan to trade our way back to the Sabine. Everything sold including the hides and pelts. Nick negotiated a good price for the sixteen mules we planned to sell. They were of much better quality than the local mules, and in high demand for the irrigated farms. A local dealer offered him $120 for the mules and $75 for each of the excess horses we had taken in trade. We had only paid $40 for the mules, but I decided to test the waters and asked $150 for the mules, and agreed to $75 on the horses. The trader looked hurt, but offered $135 which I accepted with a smile. I knew he would be able to resell them for a nice profit, but I didn't have time to try to piece out selling them one at a time, and was ready to get on the road. Grandfather Thomas Turner had always said, "A man never went broke selling for a profit." It made me smile to remember him and my family in the Carolinas. I wondered what he would have thought of Texas. I think he would have liked it, as nothing seemed to scare him or my father, and they both liked a challenge. I could not linger here any longer, and San Antonio held no charms for me. If I was going to ever move to Texas, there were things to tend to elsewhere first! Morning's first rays found us heading back toward home on the Camino Real in the company of our escort.

---

I wondered if Lieutenant Rodriquez and his troop had been sent to make sure we left or to get us safely on the road. Either way, I was glad to have them along. We imposed again on the gracious hospitality of Don Fernando. He was a man I instinctively liked, respected and trusted. We hit the trail early riding the best six of our horses and leading four pack mules, leaving our escort behind. We packed grain for the animals, as we didn't plan on giving them much time to graze on the trip back. Once we reached the Colorado, the country became greener and seemed less hostile. We camped at the shelter and pens we had built earlier. Usually we liked to get across a river before camping, but in this country, the shelter and pens were too important to ignore. The river was up a little the next morning, so we had to swim the stock across. We primed our pans with fresh powder and pushed eastward. "Uncle Charles, I think ol' Aaron here is in a hurry to get us out of Texas." Rob quipped.

"To tell the truth, Rob, I sure don't want to have to deal with any more Comanche or Karankawa. I recall Louisiana seemin' a mite more peaceable."

"'Cept when us and Ol' Hickory whupped the Red Coats." Rob added.

In a few days we had reached the muddy Brazos. It was down some from our previous crossing. The horses and mules walked belly deep all the way across. It still would have been too deep for a wagon; I made a mental note of the need for a ferry here. We camped on the east bank, and turned the horses out to graze. They were tired and so were we. We lit out early the next morning making for the Navasota. We crossed easily and camped on "my land," as I came to think of it. It felt so good to camp on this site. The next day we pulled off the trail to check on the Smiths. They were glad to see us, and Janie fixed us a big lunch of fried venison, cornbread and fried potatoes. It was good to eat a "woman cooked meal." They asked us about our travels, and caught us up to date with them. "We've had it mighty peaceful here so far this summer. We put up plenty of corn and fodder for the winter. Those heifers I caught are growing out real nice and getting pretty tame and so is that nice young bull. Next time you come through, I may have quite a herd."

Janie added, "It's not just the herd growin' neither."

We smiled and congratulated them. I worried about them in such an isolated place, so far from help. We said our good-byes and reached our previous little stockade on the Trinity. As Charles and I put the canvas roof back on the poles, he caught my attention. "Major, you better go see about Cody."

I looked up to see him throwing up his lunch in the grass, shaking like a leaf. "Cody, you sick?"

"No sir, not exactly. You remember what happened here?" Of course I did. This was where we had barely survived a bloody fight with the Karankawa, and Cody had nearly been killed with a glancing blow from an arrow to the head. "Major, in my sleep sometimes I still hear them screamin'. I was pretty scared then, and I still am."

"Cody, look at me son. We were all terrified. Shoot, I'm still scared just talking about it. There is a sight less Karankawa here than there used to be. We thinned 'em out a bit. You are one tough kid, Owl Killer." I gave him a quick hug around the shoulders and turned to walk away so he would not see the tears glistening in my own eyes. I had no more words of comfort or wisdom. I had led this group into serious trouble twice. I was as scared as he was but couldn't let him see that. We passed a restless night there. Perhaps it was the ghosts of the Karankawa that haunted our sleep. When morning came, I was ready to be somewhere else.

Once across the Trinity, the pines again came to dominate the landscape. We continued pushing eastward, riding long and late, resting little. When we finally reached Nacogdoches, I saw the arrogant young Lieutenant Don Luis Hernandez y Mendoza. I sorely wanted to teach that pup a lesson, but my better judgment prevailed. I sent the rest of our party on to the Campos farm while I paid my respects to the alcalde. He received me well, and I gave him a condensed version of our travels. "Your Excellency, our trip could not have succeeded without your gracious assistance." I placed a gold escudo in his hand, along with the required ten peso fee. "I hope we will be welcome on our return."

"Texas needs more men like you, Mr. Turner. I would be honored to have you as a resident of our province."

"Your Excellency, would it be possible to buy a parcel of raw land in your district?"

"Yes. I am allowed to issue claims to worthy settlers. There are fees, of course."

I saw the same greedy smile spread across his face as I described the land I wanted.

"I can grant to you a league and a labor, if you intend to both ranch and farm. Are you a Catholic in good standing? But of course you are. Tell me the boundaries, as best as you know them." His goose quill scratched away hurriedly as I described the property. "There will be a filing fee of one hundred pesos, plus a registration fee to enter it into our records of five pesos. Are you in a hurry?"

I smiled as I understood. "Yes. How much would it take to expedite the paper work?"

"Perhaps another gold escudo for such a choice property would not seem too much?" I nodded my assent. He called for his assistants, and the two of them completed the necessary forms and embossed them with a heavy seal. The clerk then produced a huge, heavy leather bound book. Turning to the appropriate page, the alcalde and I both entered our signatures, and I also signed the land grant. The clerk carefully took the one hundred and five pesos. I handed the mordida to the alcalde, and decided it would not be a bad thing to keep myself in the good graces of the clerks.

"May I reward your clerks for such good service?" He nodded his approval. The astonished clerks looked at the ten pesos I handed each of them like a vast treasure, a huge smile spreading across their faces. As the ink dried, they presented me with the documents on the highest quality paper, sealed in a canvas envelope, which was then wrapped in an oiled leather pouch. A duplicate was kept there, plus the entry in the book of records.

I owned land in Texas A league and a labor amounted to more than 4000 acres. How long would it be before I could fulfill my dream? I was burning to be on my way.

The Campos let us put our stock in their corral where we fed them an extra ration of grain and turned them out in a rail fenced pasture behind the cabin. Mrs. Campos fixed us a supper of beans and corn tortillas. I noticed the lack of meat and said nothing. Looking in their smoke house after supper, I found it bare. We had more than enough side-meat to last us all the way home, so I gave them two sides of smoked pork and a peso each for their kindness.

We had a quick breakfast of corn tortillas, beans and fried salt pork, then headed east on the Camino Real. That night we stayed at the Caddo village of Man Who Laughs. They treated us well and told of their shooting exploits with the new rifled muskets. When we departed I gave our host another horn of powder and a pouch of shot.

As I rode down the trail, I realized we had made some friends in Texas. There were the Caddo of Man Who Laughs village, the Campos, the Waco and Tonkawa Indians, the Smiths, and Don Fernando. It was a good start. I could feel the leather bound packet inside my shirt. It made me smile. We pushed the animals hard and crossed the Sabine at dusk. Wheeling my horse around in mid-stream, I took a long look at Texas in the fading light. Texas was my "promised land." I would be back.

# 9

## December 1817, Turner's Crossing, Marlboro County, South Carolina

CHRISTMAS 1817 FOUND me visiting my family in South Carolina. Mother spoiled me pretty well, and invited all my siblings and their families for Christmas dinner. It was so good to be home again. I found myself the center of attention as everyone wanted to hear about the grand Texas expedition. It was hard to know where to begin the story of a lifetime. They sat entranced during the tales of our Indian encounters, especially the cannibalistic Karankawa and the fearless Comanche. I don't think they noticed the tremor in my hands as I relived those moments. I opened the oiled leather pouch and canvas envelope to show them the elaborately written and sealed deed to my 4,000 acre land grant. They were stunned at the sheer size, and amused that I had to declare myself a "good Catholic." I reminded them that, technically, "catholic" meant "universal," and I was certainly a member of the "universal body of Christ." I smiled as they gradually recognized my delicate use of words. When I talked of Texas, it became a magical kingdom, a Garden of Eden, the "promised land." The Camino Real transformed from a rutted wagon track to a highway paved with gold. In many ways, Texas was all these things, but with a dark, untamed side. As the children of Israel fought to inherit the land of the covenant, Texas would yield its legacy only to blood, sweat, and tears. In time, I would come to know the full price of its treasures.

---

Upon returning to Savannah I met a beautiful widow, Nancy King, with three children. Her husband had been a casualty of the recent war. The children were Lucius, Louisa, and Marcus. I had met them when I had filled the pulpit as a substitute minister at a small rural Methodist church. Nancy had invited me to Sunday dinner each of the six weeks I had preached there. No one would ever claim that Nancy was an extraordinary beauty, although she was an attractive woman. She was tall and graceful, but there was an aura about her that drew me to her. She was the type of person who could rise to any challenge, who was possessed of tremendous self-confidence which was contagious to me. When I was around her, I felt ten feet tall. Her smile became the sunshine of my days, the moonlight of my nights. I had fallen in love.

I made a visit to see Aaron, Jr., and the step-children. Aaron did not know me, and cried when I approached him. The step-children hardly acknowledged my presence. There was no doubt that chapter of my life was sealed closed, never to be reopened.

Would I be making the same mistake marrying a widow

with children? While Cynthia's death had officially ended our marriage, my relationship with her children had doomed it from the beginning. This would be the key with Nancy. I had a long talk with her. We both wanted to marry, but it was agreed it must be with the blessing of her children.

I spent what time I could spare getting to know the kids. All three enjoyed fishing. There was a mill pond near Nancy's home which the five of us would visit with fishing poles and a picnic basket. They delighted in catching sunfish, which we threw back to catch again another day. Louisa loved to climb into my lap and read a book with me. She was smart as a whip, as were her brothers. As spring passed into summer, it was obvious the children approved of me, and I adored them. It was time to approach the children about the subject of marriage. To my great relief, they were delighted! Nancy had no close relatives from whom to seek their blessing, and we were both of age to know our own minds. In a simple ceremony, we were married in September 1818 by a justice of the peace. I was 34; she was 30. I had entered the relationship that would bless and sustain me the rest of my life.

―――――――

I continued to make recurring trading voyages from Savannah. The trips seemed longer, and I hurried the sails along by sheer force of will power to hasten my return. I had written my parents to tell them of my marriage to Nancy. They had responded to invite us to visit them for Christmas.

Nancy and the children had never been to sea. We sailed from Savannah to Georgetown on one of the company's coastal traders. The seas were calm, and we made the voyage in a day and a night to arrive at Widyah Bay.

Lucius, now a growing twelve year old, noticed the sign at the docks. "Father, it says 'Turner Shipping and Trade.' Isn't that the same company you work for in Savannah?"

"Yes, son, it is. They have offices all over both sides of the Atlantic."

"I didn't know it was such a big company. It says 'Josiah Turner, Founder.' Is he related to you?"

"Yes. That is my great-grandfather. I never knew him. But you would have liked my grandfather, Thomas Turner. He was a good, brave man who loved children. You will like my father, Thomas, Junior, and my mother, too. They are excited you are coming for Christmas."

The other two children had been listening. Louisa asked, "Papa Aaron, do you own the company?"

"Well, yes and no. It was started by my great-grandfather, and it belongs to his grandchildren and great-grandchildren. I do own a small part of it."

We spent the night in the second story apartment above the company offices, and we departed on a company scow early the next morning. The slaves pulled hard against the great oak oars, rowing in rhythm to the cadence of a chant known only to them. It was ghostly to hear it again. I pointed out items of interest as we traveled up the Pee Dee. A rising breeze allowed the scow to set a lug sail to hasten our journey, but the wind felt raw and cold.

Arriving at Cheraw Landing, we found my brother, James, waiting with a wagon pulled by a fine pair of draft horses. He welcomed us all warmly, as I made the round of introductions. We loaded into the wagon, which had the canvas fastened to the bows. There were several wool blankets to wrap Nancy and the children and to cushion them against the bumps in the road. I sat on the wagon box with James, enjoying our visit as we trotted along to Turner's Crossing. Mother and Father made a special effort to make Nancy and the children feel welcome. There was a jug of cold milk with a plate of fresh gingerbread men waiting in the kitchen.

The whole extended family gathered for Christmas dinner so Nancy and the kids got to meet everyone else. Father recited his expected litany of requested stories of family history for the grandchildren. I enjoyed hearing them again as much as the little ones.

James and I rode up to check on my farm the day after Christmas. Mr. Hoodarm, the tenant, had been able to buy the property joining it. He was very interested in buying the farm. He offered me $300 for the fifty-nine acres with its cabin and barns. It had been a gift from Grandfather Thomas. I had never lived on it or developed any particular attachment to it. I accepted his offer. We met the next day at the bank in Turner's Crossing. The district clerk's office kept a branch office there at the bank, so we were able to complete the transaction. The 300 silver coins felt good in the leather bag. I knew it would help get my start in Texas. But selling the property cut one more tie to South Carolina. I was now another step closer to my dream.

---

By April 1819, the Caribbean trading season had begun in earnest. I would have more than usual to occupy my thoughts during my travels. Nancy had confided that she was with child, due sometime in September. By May, when we arrived in New Orleans, we learned that there had been a collapse of the banking system in the United States. With little or no oversight of banks, many had made questionable loans to family and friends, resulting in the collapse of one bank after another. Those banks that had issued paper money without adequate backing in hard assets were hardest hit. Their paper was worthless. The credit system collapsed. Commerce only continued when one was able to pay with coin or resort to the age old system of barter. Turner Shipping and Trade remained solvent, but without letters of credit, it was nearly impossible to conduct business. Charles Contois and I paid a visit to the company attorney in New Orleans, Joseph Hawkins.

Hawkins introduced us to a young man who had come to study the law under him. His name would be one I would never forget: Stephen F. Austin. I recognized the family name from our previous dealings with the lead mines of his father, Moses Austin. Stephen told us the financial crisis had caused his father's creditors to foreclose the mine to cover debts. Stephen had been left nearly penniless, with his father's creditors pressing him for payment. Moses had gone to Texas to seek permission to establish a colony of 300 settlers. This immediately caught my attention. He had little more information, but promised to stay in contact with me.

Rob joined the rest of us for supper. He was his usual robust self. "Well, Major, there is no point in going up river to Natchitoches. Trading there is at a standstill unless you've got coin in your pocket. Nobody ain't selling nothin'."

Austin's curiosity was piqued. "Excuse me. Did you say 'Major'?"

"Yes, sir. Ol' Aaron here was a full blown major of volunteers against the British at the Battle of New Orleans. I was a captain, and Uncle Charles here was a lieutenant. General Andy Jackson ran the whole show. I don't think we could have whipped 'em by ourselves."

The reserved Austin didn't seem to know what to make of Rob. Sometimes we didn't either.

"The Major, he knows practically everything there is to know about Texas since we went tradin' down there in Eighteen seventeen. We made friends with some of the Mexicans and even some of the Indians, too. He knows a full bird colonel down at Vera Cruz. The Major has got him a Spanish land grant for more than four thousand acres down on the Navasota River."

Austin and Hawkins exchanged a glance. "We would like to discuss this more with you," Austin said in a dead serious tone.

We talked about Texas late into the night, including geography, Indians, trade, and the importance of the Camino Real. Austin summarized the political situation. The rebels pushing for the independence of Mexico from Spain had stubbornly persevered in the remote areas. Their cause was far from dead. Stephen's father was dealing with the officials appointed by Spain in San Antonio. Our friend, Santa Anna, was still a person of great influence all along the eastern coast of Mexico, who staunchly supported the Royalist cause. The United States and Spain had just signed the Adams-Onis Treaty, confirming the Sabine River as the international boundary. Moses Austin was seeking a land grant from east of the Brazos to west of the Colorado to settle 300 families. I sensed that Stephen had doubts about his father's ability to obtain the grant, and even more concerns about the ability to finance such a huge undertaking. At the very least, he had my full attention.

As we left, Rob, Charles and I talked about the prospects for Austin's Colony. It seemed like a tall order. But if it could be done, it would have tremendous potential. We wrapped up our remaining affairs in New Orleans and boarded *Liberty* for our voyage home.

---

I was home in time for the birth of Joseph, the first child born to our marriage. He was a feisty little boy with brown hair, blue eyes and dimples. His birth united us as a family even more than I had hoped. The children doted on their baby brother. It was a wonder the boy ever learned to walk, as he was carried everywhere he went. He had a bubbly personality that endeared him to all of us.

The early months of 1820 were still financially uncertain, but gradually improving. The $300 from the sale of my farm helped us manage very well. I again took the pulpit in our village until the trading season resumed.

When we called in Havana, we learned there had been significant changes in Spain. King Ferdinand VII had abolished the legislature and suspended the Constitution of 1814. His encroachment on the rights of Spaniards had led to open revolt in Spain in 1820. The King had been forced to reinstate the Constitution of 1814 and the legislature. Special privileges of the Catholic Church were reduced, and foreigners were allowed to own land within Spanish territory.

These changes encouraged the independence movement

in Mexico. New converts to the concept of independence from the upper and middle classes in Mexico turned to conservative Spanish Colonel Augustin de Iturbide to consolidate their movement. Mexico was split three ways. The original liberal revolutionary forces held on tenuously in the south, west, and the northern mountains. The newer conservative independence movement gained momentum in the cities, among large land owners, business interests, and dissatisfied former Royalists. Mexico City and the Gulf coast were Royalist enclaves. The two independence movements did not unite and distrusted each other. In the province of Texas, there were isolated pockets of dedicated Royalists, but there was wide-spread support for independence from Spain.

Weeks later, as we approached the harbor of Vera Cruz, there was a strong sense of turmoil. I was concerned about the continued viability of our trade in Mexico, so I requested a meeting with Santa Anna. It was granted the same day.

"Your Excellency, I trust you are well."

"Yes, I am well, Major Turner, but I suspect my health is of little concern to you. How may I help you?"

I was surprised by his bluntness. "Colonel, I am aware of the unrest in Mexico, and am concerned about how it may affect our trade here."

"It seems wealth and power are the root of most desires, does it not? As long as I am in command here, your trading position is secure. I have not forgotten your previous service to me. However, there is once again a need for your assistance. I am well supplied with rifle and cannon shot, but there is an acute need for gunpowder. Are you interested in immediately transporting a large amount to me here?"

Here was an opportunity I had not foreseen. "Yes, Excellency. However, the merchants in Kingston will not sell on credit. I must pay them in gold or silver on delivery. Are you prepared to trust me with your King's treasure?"

"Major Turner, I have always found you a man of your word. I would, of course, expect a written contract. Captain Avila has already prepared such a document."

I smiled at his foresight. He had known I would not turn him down. "How much would be required?"

"As much gunpowder as can be bought with ten thousand ounces of silver."

I blinked, as this truly was a vast amount of cargo. "Yes. It can be done."

We set all the sail *Liberty* would carry for Kingston. When we arrived, our shipping office quickly and quietly bought the gunpowder at a bargain price for the hard currency. Having bought all the gunpowder available, there was still money left. I purchased cases of .69 caliber muskets and shot, hoping Santa Anna could use them. The *Ghost of Savannah* was in port and pressed into service to carry the rest of the cargo. Captain Marion still commanded her. We would sail on the morning tide.

With such a dangerous cargo, we avoided all strange sail. We couldn't risk a skirmish with a pirate schooner with our holds full of gunpowder. The weather was kind to us. We could feel the ghost of the old *Agnes* sailing with us. We had an unspoken fear of a recurrence of that disaster. We docked at the island fortress in the harbor of Vera Cruz sooner than we had expected. The red and gold flag of Spain still flew over the fortress. Captain Avila met us at the fortress and took us immediately to Santa Anna.

"Gentlemen, you have served me well once again. I will not forget your fidelity."

———

When we arrived in New Orleans, we found the *Samuel Brown* docked at Turner Shipping and Trade. Rob was in the office with Charles. "Well, Aaron, we're glad you could come see us. How is your friend, Colonel Fancy Pants?"

"I swear, Rob. You never change! I guess I'm glad to see both of you anyway. And our trading partner, Colonel Santa Anna, is quite well."

"Major, our friend Austin is in town. Could you come with us to Joseph Hawkins' house to meet with him over supper and a bottle of wine?"

My dreams of Texas again moved closer to reality. The time to act would be soon. As I walked back to our quarters, I saw a single brilliant falling star, briefly lighting the sky from east to west. In spite of the New Orleans heat, a chill ran down my spine. I soon would be following that star west to my destiny.

# 10

## January 1821, Savannah, Georgia

WHEN I RETURNED TO Savannah, I found Nancy far along with child. Her letters had not caught up with me, although she had received mine. In January 1821, she gave birth to Mary Anne, our dark-eyed beautiful baby girl. It was so good to be home with Nancy and the children. Joseph had grown so much. Once he realized who I was, he toddled to me, holding out his arms while declaring "Daddy!" It melted my heart to hear it, making me ache to realize how much I had missed while I was gone. Lucius, Louisa and Marcus had all grown. They seemed so glad to have me home.

I did a little preaching, performed a couple of weddings and a funeral while waiting for trading season to begin. The economy had stabilized and hard money was circulating again. Letters of credit from the larger, more stable banks were traded at only a small discount from their face value. Many of the small or less credit-worthy banks had closed, never to reopen. I received a letter from Joseph Hawkins asking me to meet with him as soon as I reached New Orleans. Something in the tone of his letter sounded enthusiastic, and I must admit, it was highly contagious.

---

Joseph Hawkins' voiced boomed from his study. "Aaron! Charles! Welcome! I have great news! Moses Austin has had his proposal approved by the alcalde of San Antonio. We lack only the signature of the Viceroy. He is already recruiting settlers. Are you interested?"

Charles quickly spoke up, "My job is here, but I'll help you get it going."

I sat smiling and thinking. "Joseph, do the Austin's have adequate finances to make this work?"

"I have committed most of my own money to this venture in return for a large land grant. Stephen is raising money as we speak."

"You know I already have land on the Navasota River. Would the Austin Colony recognize my title?"

"I already have a signed document recognizing your prior claim and your right to be considered part of the colony. In addition, you are eligible for an additional grant. It would three hundred and twenty acres of farm land, six hundred and forty acres of grazing land, two hundred more for Nancy, and a hundred for each of your five children. That would be one thousand six hundred and sixty acres at twelve and a half cents per acre, or a little over two hundred dollars. Of course, it would be platted to join your own land."

"Joseph, you've got a deal. As I know Austin needs cash, I'll pay mine now. I want to see this thing work."

———————

We found Captain Rob and made a quick run to Natchitoches. I explained my plans to him on the trip. He expressed interest in taking up a claim where the Camino Real crossed the Brazos. "Major, there is a big need for a ferry there. One day when the country builds up it would be a dandy place for a steam boat landing. I'll talk to Hawkins when we get back and sign up."

We talked to Louis. He wasn't about to move, but his son and our previous guide, Chance, wanted to pick up a grant. As a single man, he would receive 960 acres. He wanted to locate it near my land on the Navasota. We found Nick and Cody Teel. Nick was now married to a pretty Creole girl named Kassandra. Cody was still just seventeen, but he would be eighteen by the time we moved. They were both in on the deal. They wanted to take up land on the Navasota. Cody said "I'll take land anywhere I can get it, except where them Karankawa tried to kill me."

We decided that Rob, Chance and the Teel brothers would go with me to get cabins built and a few acres cleared. Rob and I would leave them there, then in a few months return with the rest of our supplies. Kassie would come with us then, as would Nancy and the children.

———————

Selling Nancy on the idea wasn't hard. "Aaron, I can't think of anything more exciting! If Texas is half as grand as you say, it must be heaven on earth."

I detected a sense of sarcasm in her smiling face. "Well, I know I lay it on a little thick about Texas. But it is an amazing place. I'm drawn to it like a moth to a flame. Are you willing to accept the risks with me?"

"Oh, I think I had better, especially since you are going to be a father again."

"When?"

"Right around Christmas. Are you taking your baby into such an awful place?"

I paused. "You know, maybe we should reconsider."

She smiled. "You'll be lonely."

"What do you mean, 'lonely'?"

"I'm going to Texas with or without you!" Nancy laughed.

---

I tried to think of all the many things we would need in Texas. When we returned to New Orleans, I found Rob and Charles. Rob was as excited as I was. I bought a sturdy wagon that was delivered to the *Samuel Brown*. We loaded boxes and barrels of corn meal, flour, lard, beans, salt pork, dried beef, coffee, sugar, dried fruit, salt and spices. We bought sacks of corn, seed corn, oats and vegetable seeds. Basic house wares were not hard to find. We bought axes, hatchets, saws, hammers, nails and other hand tools. We bought a steel plow with interchangeable blades, the parts to build a harrow, and good quality harness. Finally, we bought shot for the guns, extra flint, repair parts, and plenty of high quality powder. We steamed our way up the Mississippi to the Red River on to Natchitoches by September. The first mate was to return to pick us up in December. He was a reliable man who could be counted on to do what was expected of him. Louis, Chance, Nick, Kassie, and Cody were there to meet us. Nick had picked up four fine mules for the wagon, and some good saddle mares for us to ride. We bought a last few items and were ready to go.

The next morning, Chance's mother shed a few tears, but he was a grown man who knew how to handle himself. Mrs. Teel cried a little about Cody and Nick leaving, as did Kassie. But it was time for them to leave the nest. Kassie would be joining Nick in a few months. We set off west as the first rays of sunlight drove away the river fog. We were on the Camino Real, heading for Texas.

---

We reached the Sabine an hour before dark. Chance found the water was not too deep and the river bed firm. He rode across first, as Rob and I waited behind the wagon. Cody whipped the mules into action with words that would have made his mother blush. The wagon lurched forward into the green water and reached the sloping west bank. The mules dug in with a will and pulled the wagon up onto the level ground. Rob and I followed on horseback, accompanied by the Teel's hunting dogs. We were in Texas!

The next morning, soon after we were on the trail, a ragged looking group of unkempt men in greasy buckskins and riding thin horses appeared from the trees in front of us. They looked like hard men, thin, mean and down on their luck. As the four in front of us spread out across the narrow road, two more closed behind us. Rob and I wheeled our horses to face them. The leader of this pack of flea-bitten wolves spoke up. "Howdy, boys! Nice day for travelin'." As he spoke, they all eased their horses closer to us. Cody set the wagon brake, as both he and Nick leveled loaded double-barreled shotguns at them.

Chance, who had been carrying his rifle across his saddle, leveled it at the leader. "Y'all drop your guns and get off your horses before I blow ol' whiskers face off!"

We had our rifles trained on the two behind the wagon at close range. "Drop 'em!" I threatened in a dead earnest voice.

"Now boys, we just want some fresh horses. Thought we might trade with ya." Like a flash, he raised a pistol at Chance, but Chance put a .50 ball through his face. Cody and Nick both fired as Chance did, each knocking a man dead from the saddle with buckshot. The fourth man was already on Nick with an "Arkansas toothpick." Cody blew him into oblivion with the second barrel of his shotgun. The men behind the wagon charged straight at us with drawn saddle pistols when the gunfire started. We shot them both dead.

Just as we thought it was over, four more men appeared from both sides of the woods. One fired at me, but narrowly missed. He managed to get to the extra mares tied to the wagon. The knife in his hand flashed down to cut the lead ropes of the terrified horses. I fired the second barrel of my .45 Manton, wounding him in the side. He drew a pistol from his belt. Rob dropped him with buck and ball from his .69 caliber saddle pistol. Nick used his unfired second barrel to drop another man who tried to cut the mules free from the wagon. The other three men ran desperately into the woods north of the road.

The mules had reared and kicked, but the wagon brake held them until Cody quieted them. The mares had pulled back and broken their lead ropes, but were easily caught. The dogs charged into the woods in search of the survivors who could be heard crashing in the woods in head-long flight. We all reloaded, expecting a second attack.

We had been lucky. These had been desperate men to attack a party of our size. Of the ten attackers, seven lay in the red dust of the Camino Real. We gathered four of their malnourished horses, but two had run away east along the road. We dragged the bodies off the trail and collected their weapons. They were mostly old smooth bore muskets and saddle pistols. Their morrals were empty of food, but contained extra shot and powder. We unsaddled their horses and tied them in a line behind the wagon, throwing their saddles and tack in the bed. We didn't take time to bury them, as we felt we were still in danger. The dogs returned uninjured and empty-handed. Cody stepped into the edge of the woods to throw up. Chance appeared as cool as a winter morning until I noticed his hands shaking. Then I noticed my own trembling hands.

"Well boys, welcome back to Texas! Let's ride!"

_____

We traveled on to a good campsite and picketed the livestock. Our newly acquired horses ate like there was no tomorrow. At least they wouldn't founder on grass. None of us was hungry. We ate some jerky and parched corn, washed down with a little coffee. We hardly talked around the fire that night, but no one seemed to want to sleep. I suddenly realized that Nancy and the children could have been in that wagon. What was I doing moving them into this wild, lawless, unclaimed land?

Our next night was much more pleasant. We had arrived at the homestead of Pedro and Juanita Campos outside of Nacogdoches. We fed the stock some grain, then turned them into the pasture behind the corrals. After a fine meal, we bedded down on fresh hay in their loft.

Rob and I rode into Nacogdoches the next morning to meet with the alcalde. This time he did not keep us waiting, but treated us like visiting dignitaries. We presented him the claims for our land in Austin's Colony. Without question, he signed and sealed duplicate copies of all five claims. We paid the fee of one peso per claim. We waited as his clerks hurriedly entered our claims in the large leather bound volume of records. We read everything for accuracy and signed each document and each volume entry. I gave a mordida of a peso to both of the clerks and pressed a gold escudo in the alcalde's hand. "Mr. Turner, I know that a man of your stature will obey all the laws of the province of Texas, and that all of you are good Catholics."

I hedged and said, "We are all children of the same God. We will work hard and cause you no trouble. I know this is a land that is difficult to govern. If you ever find the need of my assistance, I will do whatever I can."

He gave an understanding nod and returned our sealed papers.

"Aaron what is this 'mordida' you mentioned?"

"It means 'little bite.' It is like a small bribe or a tip for better service. It prevents some headaches and can buy friends when you need them."

"How much is that gold escudo worth you gave your 'friend' back there?"

"Sixteen pesos. And gold is very scarce here. That is probably two months wages for the alcalde. I think it bought some good will."

"We're gonna need it in this place."

When we returned to the Campos farm we decided to rest the stock the remainder of the day. The extra grazing and rest wouldn't hurt them. I rustled in the wagon and found the best of the .69 caliber muskets and a fairly good saddle pistol of the same caliber, with a couple of flasks of powder and pouches of shot. I gave these to Pedro. Two of the extra horses were geldings that would be decent horses if given adequate care. Both would make suitable saddle horses and could do some farm work. I let Pedro take his pick of the two. After some protesting of my generosity, he selected the larger of the two which might be a little better as a farm horse. He was a big brown horse about six years old. I gave him the saddle and tack, too, along with salt, sugar, and coffee for Juanita. Their joy was hard to contain, making us all feel better considering the past few days. We left early the next day after a big breakfast. As we left, Juanita handed me a morral of corn tortillas and parched corn. At least we had a few friends in Texas.

# 11

Fall 1821, Trinity River crossing,
Camino Real, eastern Texas

TWO DAYS LATER, WE
crossed the Trinity and found remnants of our former
campsite. All of us were quiet as we remembered
the night of terror when we had been attacked by
the Karankawa. Cody was especially subdued and
seemed understandably uncomfortable. He had
suffered the most that night.

The pole corrals needed just a little repair to be
usable. It was obvious the pens had been used not
too long ago as evidenced by the presence of dried
horse droppings. The frame of the shelter was still
standing where we had endured our desperate fight.
The grass within it was trampled down, and there
were remnants of campfires near the little "fort." We
spread a heavy canvas tarp across the uprights and
lashed it in place. The wagon was backed across the
corner formed by the pens and the shelter. The ghosts

of this place haunted our sleep. We were glad to be on our way at dawn.

We turned off the road to check on Asa and Janie Smith. Asa came in from picking corn, and Janie appeared on the porch, a baby in her arms and a toddler hiding behind her skirt.

"Y'all stay to dinner. We been wantin' some company!"

"Only if you let us work for our lunch." Rob said. As soon as the animals were tended, the five of us joined Asa in the corn field. With all of us working, it wasn't long until the patch was picked, the corn shucked and the crib filled.

"You fellas sure come in handy. We had a pretty decent summer and crop. It gets lonely here, so we're mighty glad for company."

After a lunch of beans, cabbage and corn bread, we gathered up the stock to go. Our plans would put our cabins about 15 miles from the Smith's place, making us their closest neighbors. I gave Asa one of the smoothbore muskets and saddle pistols. A little extra fire power in this country could make a lot of difference.

Just before dark we reached our new home on the Navasota. We made a quick scouting ride around the perimeter to look for any signs of trouble, but everything looked peaceful.

We picketed the horses after feeding and watering them. A large tarp was extended from the side of the wagon to provide a sleeping shelter. I could feel excitement in the air as we talked late into the night.

"First, we got to get a cabin built. I already got the spot picked. I want it one hundred yards back from the road and one hundred yards back from the edge of the woods along the river."

Nick questioned, "Why so far back? There is a good spot

down there near where the woods meet the road."

Chance knew the answer. "We don't want to be caught by surprise. Most folks around here carry smooth bore muskets, not rifles like ours. They have a hard time hittin' a barn at one hundred yards. Same thing with the Indians. Their bows, even the Karankawa, aren't much good past one hundred yards, either. If we are way out here in the open, they're gonna have heck sneakin' up on us." At the mention of the Karankawa, Cody grabbed the left side of his head.

"Chance is right. As we cut the logs for the cabin, we need to get temporary corrals built for the livestock near the cabin site. We can build them from the branches we trim off the cabin logs. We need to get a cabin up where the three of you can winter and get ready for the rest of us to come in the spring."

Our night passed quickly, and we woke to bacon frying and corn cakes in the skillet. The morning dawned crisp, dry and fresh. We staked out the location of the cabin. It was to be twelve by twenty-four feet. The only door was to face the north, away from the road. Rifle ports would be cut into every wall.

Cody and Nick took the mules and wagon down to the river where they loaded rocks to use for the foundation and chimney. After they unloaded them, they set the shelter up again. We found some cypress trees in the low ground near the river that would be perfect for the bottom row of the walls. Cypress was very rot resistant. We got the trees cut and trimmed, then let the big mares drag them to the cabin site. We got the rocks placed to make a foundation for the lowest logs. We then cut and notched the sleepers all the way around so they fit tightly together. We drilled holes where the notched logs overlapped and pounded in black locust pegs to keep the logs from shifting. The wide flaring bases of the cypress trees were saved to be cut into shingles. Cody and Nick built the chimney while the rest of us cut and shaped the logs for the walls.

We kept the stock in the corral at night, but let them graze hobbled in the deep grass during the day. We had pushed them hard, and they needed the rest and the feed.

Soon, we had a split pine puncheon floor. The walls were built of peeled and trimmed pine logs up eight feet high. We cut them to build around the fireplace and door frame. We didn't take the time to square the logs as we had on our home place cabin in South Carolina. They wouldn't fit as tightly, but would serve our purposes. Post oak logs made good rafters, and when split, were used as the horizontals to which we nailed the cypress shingles. We nailed on the last shingle on the tenth day. Chance had painstakingly sawed two inch thick pine boards to build a sturdy door. He hung the door with rawhide hinges and set heavy oak bars to secure it from the inside.

We built bed frames out of post oak and rawhide straps as well as a passable table and pair of benches. There was a good source of heavy red clay south along the river. It was mixed with gravel, straw and wood ashes to chink the gaps between the logs. Rifle ports were simple to chisel out between the logs. Each rifle port was closed with large rocks or blocks of wood that could be removed only from the inside. After some final smoothing of the wooden floor, the cabin was ready to occupy.

I began to wonder about Nancy and the kids. I hoped I would not miss the birth of our next child. Nick confided in me he was really missing Kassie. He admitted it would be dangerous for her to try to winter here. "Major, being married really changes things. I don't want Cody to know how bad I'm missing her; he would really ride me about it. You missin' your family, too?"

"My friend, I miss them more than I can tell you. I can't wait to get them here, but I want it to be safe when they do arrive."

We laid out and built another cabin identical to the first one fifty feet to the north, except its door faced the south, toward the first cabin. Since we knew what were doing, we had it up in a week. The Teel brothers moved into the second cabin, although we took all our meals together.

We cut and peeled six to eight inch diameter oak logs and set them firmly upright in the ground joining the west walls of the two cabins with a palisade. We sharpened the top of each log, making the palisade about ten feet tall. We built a frame to support a roof eight feet wide and sectioned it off into stalls about every eight feet. The front sides of the stalls were built stout enough to prevent scared livestock from jumping over or breaking through the sides. Rifle ports were cut into the palisade every eight feet. Lofts for storing feed and hay were built above the stalls. Now we could really secure the livestock at night.

Finally, we hand dug a well near the cabins and lined it with river rock. We hit good water at sixteen feet and dug down four feet deeper. We built a rock wall around the well to keep out run-off and put a roof over it to keep the birds from fouling the water. An iron pulley was fastened to the roof joists, and a rope was attached to a bucket. Within a few days, the well settled enough for us to see that it would be good sweet water.

Rob took Cody with him and rode over to where the Camino Real crossed the Brazos. He got ideas about where he wanted to locate his ferry and cabin, but he wouldn't build them until next year. He even planned to have a steamboat landing there some day. When they returned, I showed them which acres I wanted them to plow and harrow. If they had time, I had brought oat seed and some early season vegetable seeds for them to sow. We left the mules and good mares with them. For our trip home, we took the remaining two geldings we had captured from the bandits. With some time, proper care and food, they had made good horses. We filled our morrals and saddle bags with provisions for our trip. We struck out east along the Camino Real the first week of November.

_____

We found the *Samuel Brown* waiting for us in Natchitoches. After quick reports to Kassie, the Teel family and Louis, we headed down river to New Orleans. Captain Rob was obviously back in his element on the bridge of his steamer. He docked us at the Turner Shipping and Trade offices right outside of Charles' office. Charles wasted no time in telling us there was urgent news for us at Joseph Hawkins' office.

We gave Hawkins a brief summary of our efforts and showed him our signed and sealed documents from Nacogdoches.

Hawkins seemed to linger over these. "Gentlemen, our ship of fate sails on troubled waters." He proceeded to explain the changing situation in Mexico. The Spanish Viceroy had sent a trusted officer, General Augustin Iturbide, to fight a rebel army under Vicente Guerrero at the village of Iguala near Acapulco. Rather than fight, the two men joined forces declaring for independence. They had issued the "Plan of Iguala" with three stated guarantees. First, there must be complete independence from Spain. Second, Roman Catholicism would be the official state religion of Mexico. Finally, there would be the equality of men of all races. They devised a flag of green, white and red to represent these three principles. Whole military garrisons joined them, as did city after city. Only the fortresses at Acapulco and Vera Cruz remained in Royal hands. The Viceroy and Iturbide concluded the Treaty of Cordoba recognizing the independence of Mexico. Spain disavowed the treaty and the Viceroy was declared a traitor to Spain. Iturbide was made the head of a provisional government.

"What of our friend Santa Anna?" I asked.

"As usual, he has proven an astute politician and declared for Iturbide. Our grants, and yours, were made by the government of Spain. It remains to see if the government of Mexico will recognize them. At this point, all we can do is pray that they will."

# 12

## December 1821, Savannah, Georgia

                I ARRIVED IN SAVANNAH
to find that I was already a father. Our daughter,
Francis, had been impatient, arriving three weeks
ahead of schedule. I felt guilty for missing her delivery,
but Nancy knew it couldn't be helped. As she rocked
and nursed Francis by the fire, we talked late into the
night about Texas. I expressed my concerns for the
safety of Nancy and the children.

    "Aaron, I love you. I would follow you to the
ends of the earth. But Texas is your dream and seems
to be your destiny. I want to be part of your dream
as it becomes reality. I could die of fever in Georgia,
be struck by lightning anywhere, or be killed by
an Indian in Texas. I'm not afraid. I want to live at
your side, and if God wills it, to die there, too." I was
speechless. I held her and the baby in my arms as if I
would never let them go.

    We sold Nancy's home and made the necessary

arrangements for our departure. Nancy carefully wrapped fruit tree seedlings in damp moss and canvas. She chose her favorite vegetable seeds and placed them in waxed paper envelopes in oiled leather pouches. She packed the kitchen goods, clothes bedding and, especially, the handmade quilts. She was practical, taking only those things appropriate for such a primitive environment. She packed primers, slates, chalk and books to continue the children's education.

Most of the things I needed would be acquired in New Orleans. However, there were three special things that I would need to get elsewhere: a stallion, a bull and a jack. I bought a very fine Thoroughbred stallion. He stood sixteen and a half hands and was black as coal with a white star. I planned to breed him to the best of the native mares. I also bought an excellent Shorthorn bull to breed to the wild longhorn heifers and cows. Both the stallion and bull were expensive, but part of a long-term plan for profit. They were carefully loaded into specially built stalls in the hold of *Liberty*.

We set sail for New Orleans, with an important detour to Havana. There I bought a magnificent Spanish jack. He was long, strong, sixteen hands tall, and a rich dark bay color. We had to keep him apart from the stallion, as they had an instant deathly hatred for each other. I planned to breed him to our high quality draft mares, to produce the good mules that were in such demand.

When we arrived in New Orleans, Rob was waiting for us with the *Samuel Brown*. We bought the remainder of the supplies we needed plus some trade goods. We discovered there were several other families also heading to Austin's Colony.

Joseph Hawkins came down to the docks. "I have good

news for you. Iturbide has declared himself Emperor of Mexico, and has acknowledged the validity of our land grants. There will be several more families going with you. Some want to settle with you at Navasota Crossing, and some are going farther west. Stephen Austin and I had hoped you would agree to guide them as far as your settlement."

"Of course I will, as long as they will be under my orders as far as the settlement. Will they agree?"

"They already have," he smiled. "We had anticipated you would accept."

Our animals and goods were soon loaded on the *Samuel Brown*. Our older children were very excited. Frankly, I was more excited than they were. We met the Jamison, Parker, Morgan and Moore families. There would be more waiting at Natchitoches.

_____

Captain Rob guided the *Samuel Brown* into the landing at Natchitoches. Most of the passengers and freight had been unloaded when a tremendous concussion shook the whole town. Barrels, flaming boards, bodies of men and beasts rained down in a storm of debris and billowing smoke. The boiler on *Samuel Brown* had exploded! The wooden upper structure was burning like a furnace. Survivors were jumping off the bow and the stern. The blast had blown a hole in the bottom. The *Samuel Brown* slowly settled into the muddy water of the Red River, extinguishing the flames as it sank to the river bed.

We stood in stunned, deafened silence. Struggling survivors were helped up the slippery bank. Captain Rob had been in the bow directing the unloading of the cargo. The explosion had blown him into the water. He sat on the muddy bank with his head in his hands, sobbing quietly. The steamboat was a total loss. His long-time friend and first mate had been at the helm when the explosion occurred. All the boiler room crew had certainly died. Bodies of people and animals floated in the muddy red water. Rowboats were collecting the shattered bodies. The current would carry the carcasses of the animals down river.

I had instantly made an assessment of my family. Although horrified, they were uninjured. A boy was frantically searching for his family. "Son, let me help you."

He turned to me with tears blinding his eyes. "I wanted to be the first one off the boat, so I ran ahead. My parents, brother and sister were still on board when it blew up." He was shaking all over, as silent tears rolled down his face.

"What's your name, son?"

"Gray. Gray Jamison."

"My name's Aaron Turner. I've got some boys about your age. You wait over there with them while I look for your family." I looked at the bodies lined up along the bank. I recognized the bodies of his parents, and finally found his brother and sister. I located Mr. Moore, who confirmed that they were the Jamison family. We set their bodies aside from the others. How could I tell this boy that his whole family was dead? My heart ached for him. Then I spotted Rob stumbling among the rows of bodies. I put my arm around his shoulder and guided him to the porch of Louis' store. Louis and his wife wrapped him in a blanket and brought him a cup of hot coffee. Seeing that he was in good hands, I turned my attention to Gray.

"Gray, can I talk to you? I need you to be grown up beyond your years. Can you be brave?"

"Yes sir," he cried. "Are they dead?"

"Yes, boy. All of them."

He nodded and began to cry quietly. "Can I see them?"

I took him by the hand, leading him to all that remained of his whole world. He fell clutching his mother's body, and embraced each of the others in turn. I carried him in my arms to Nancy. She took him inside Louis' inn and put him to bed. Lucius, Louise and Marcus made pallets on the floor in the room near him. They seemed to sense the gravity of the situation. Their protective instincts were aroused toward him. They took him in as if he was their own brother.

The magnitude of the tragedy was hard to comprehend. The good people of Natchitoches dug graves for the dead and made markers for those who could be identified. I donned my ministerial black frock coat and preached a single funeral for all of them. There was little consolation to offer their surviving family members, but I tried.

Captain Rob slowly emerged from his stupor. He would finally eat and drink, but wouldn't say much. I went to him after supper the day after the funeral. "Rob, the explosion wasn't your fault. No one blames you. I'm really sorry about the loss of your friends and your boat. I don't know what to say to you. We've got to be leaving for Texas. I really need you to help me get this bunch of greenhorns safe as far as the Navasota. And folks are sure going to need that ferry across the Brazos. Won't you come with us?"

He cleared his throat, and in a weak croaking voice said, "I'm just a shell of a man. I won't be much use to you."

"Friend, I am going to need you more than you can imagine. Please help me."

He looked at me with blood-shot eyes and a hollow face. He closed his eyes and nodded his approval.

———

The wagons were loaded and the horses and mules harnessed. There would be ten wagons heading west. The Spanish jack was tied behind our wagon along with the Shorthorn bull and two Shorthorn milk cows. A young boar and three gilts were loaded in a stout crate in the wagon. I would know we were getting civilized when we could butcher and smoke our own hogs. Lard for cooking, bacon for breakfast, ham for special occasions would be an improvement over a constant diet of beef and venison. There was also a crate with a Dominique rooster and two dozen hens. There might be some eggs to go with that bacon. I rode the stallion. He was tall, tough, and ready to go. I think he could out run anything in Texas! Mr. Moore's eleven-year old son, Tanner, drove Rob's wagon for him. Rob sat on the wagon box apparently disinterested in anything around him. The Parkers and their three sons pulled in behind him. Kassie Teel, true to the country girl she was, drove her own team. She was one tough woman. There were several others in the group as we finally got strung out in driving order. A little after daylight we pulled onto the rutted Camino Real, the legendary King's Highway to Texas, the 'Promised Land.'

Traveling with a group of wagons was slower than our previous trips mounted or with only one wagon. But there was safety in numbers, and we had our wives and children. It took us two days to reach the Sabine. On March 5, 1822, we crossed into Texas. A sudden chill ran down my spine as our wagon pulled across the slowly swirling muddy red water up onto the west bank. This was our River Jordan and Texas was our "promised land." I splashed along side the wagon on the stallion. I reached up to the wagon box and grabbed Nancy's hand for a tight squeeze. Her smile spoke volumes. The other wagons made their way across until we were all firmly on Texas soil. Removing my hat, bowing my head and raising my voice, I lead us in a prayer of thanksgiving and a plea for God's protection on our journey. Our odyssey was beginning in earnest.

# 13

March, 1822, Camino Real, eastern Texas

THE THIRD NIGHT ON THE road, Man Who Laughs, and a handful of Caddo braves, trotted their horses toward our evening camp. They recognized me, and although I only spoke a little Caddo, we all spoke Spanish. We made some small talk. We didn't have much in the way of trade goods to offer. Mr. Moore was a blacksmith and gunsmith by trade. He set up his grindstone and offered to sharpen anything they needed. They had him put an edge on all their knives and steel tomahawks. They said they had some old muskets that needed to be repaired back at their village. They were aware of our route, and would try to catch up to us on the trail.

Within a few days we were stopped at the farm of Pedro Campos outside of Nacogdoches. "Amigo, it is good to se you again. Where are your wife and your children?"

I introduced them to Pedro and Juanita and

then made the round of introductions of the rest of our party. "Can we set up our wagons in your pasture and let the livestock graze?"

"Si, amigo. Welcome back. You know that we are not Spaniards anymore, but Mexicans?"

"Yes, so I have heard. Have things changed much around here?"

"Maybe so, a little. There has been fighting in other places but here it has been peaceful. There are no soldiers here any more. The arrogant young lieutenant was promoted to captain by the Spanish, but his sergeant cut his throat in the night, and the rest of the soldados went home." He laughed until he wheezed. "The alcalde, he is the best Mexican in Nacogdoches now." He gave a sly smile. I have been able to shoot a few deer with the musket you gave me. I made some harness for the horse you gave me so I can grow enough corn and beans to have plenty for us to eat and some to sell. I now have a few goats, including one Juanita milks, and a few pigs and chickens, too. We are eating a little better now."

I took the men of the group into Nacogdoches in the morning to meet the alcalde. "Mr. Turner, it is good to see you safely back in what is now the Republic of Mexico."

"Your Excellency, allow me to introduce my companions to you. They are here to settle in Austin's Colony."

Before I could continue, he interrupted. "That agreement was with Spain. This is now Mexico. I have no instructions on how the Emperor Iturbide wishes me to proceed."

It was my turn to interrupt. "You will be delighted to know that I have a copy of the edict issued by the Emperor, and embossed with his seal, confirming the grant to Stephen Austin and those other grants made in the past, including my own." I smiled slyly.

The alcalde studied the document with intense scrutiny. He ran his finger over the great seal and studied the signature.

"These men need to have their claims validated, your honor."

"I will have to think on this matter, Mr. Turner."

"Your Excellency, we must not be delayed to reach our claims. There are cabins to build and fields to plow. Perhaps the process could be expedited?" I pulled a pouch of silver pesos from my pocket, and counted out 20 pesos which I rested on the corner of his desk.

The claims were quickly signed, sealed and registered. The fees were collected, and the entries were entered in the great leather bound volume of records. Each of us initialed the entries and signed the registration forms. To be on the safe side, I re-registered my own claims with the new regime. It only cost a few more pesos, and might prevent problems later. "Alcalde, you have always dealt fairly with me. I know you do not have many soldados here to protect you. If you ever need assistance, please send a rider on a swift horse. I will come to your aid."

"Mr. Turner, I have found you also to be a man of honor and your word. I am proud that you are settling in my district. I will support you however I can, and I will call on you if the need arises."

We bid goodbye to our hosts, and made only a short day on the Camino Real. As the afternoon progressed, a frontal line of clouds appeared in the southeast. They continued to build until flashes of sheet lightning could be seen within the cloud bank. We turned into a meadow of several acres in the pine woods and set up camp. By dark, the rain was falling in sheets. By morning the rain had decreased to a heavy mist, but the road was a river of mud. As I scouted ahead, even the valiant stallion was struggling with the heavy red mud. We stayed put in our meadow another day, as the sun gradually drove away the clouds. By afternoon, the air was drying, but the road was impassable. In two days, we decided to give it a try. The wagons were able to move slowly and with great difficulty for the straining horses and mules. After five miles, the animals were spent. We found a glade of about twenty acres with a good stand of grass. The glade was on a slight high spot and drier than the surrounding area. We gave the road another day to dry while the animals rested.

We took advantage of the imposed day of rest to do minor repairs to the wagons and harness. We greased all the axles and restowed our cargo. It was hard for the women to keep the clothes and bedding dry. Nancy never complained, but made the best of things. She had the boys collect pine bows which they laid around the wagon to minimize the problems with the mud. She rigged clothes lines from the wagon to a nearby tree to air out the damp clothes and bedding. The children enjoyed the adventure, and baby Francis slept through it all. The cool dry air and sunshine felt good and made me feel a little bit lazy.

Finally, the roads were drier and we found the roadbed sandy instead of the sticky red clay. We made twelve miles that day. Man Who Laughs and several of his tribe caught up with us that night. Mr. Moore, whom we knew as Richard, was busy repairing muskets. Most were easy repairs. He was good at his trade. While his father was busy, Tanner cranked the grinding wheel, sharpening knives, axes and hatchets. The Caddo had brought a fat doe and a young buck to share with our camp. The fresh meat was a real treat. Man Who Laughs offered Richard an orphaned filly in exchange for the repairs. She was a pretty little horse, eight or nine months old, and a nice sorrel with white socks and blaze. But she would not be worth much to the Caddo. She was more likely to become a meal than a war pony.

When Tanner saw the filly, the end result was inevitable. "Dad, please take the trade!"

"Son, it's going to be a year and a half before she is ready to train. That is going to be a lot of work for us." His smile indicated he knew he had already lost the discussion.

"Dad, I'll take care of her and learn how to break her myself!" His light brown hair and pleading blue eyes made the argument pretty lop-sided.

Richard accepted the trade with the Caddo and threw in a couple of horns of powder and pouches of shot. Man Who Laughs chuckled. Speaking Spanish through me, he told Richard he had a son who was a good horse trader, too. He asked Tanner if he had a name for the horse. Indicating that he did not, Man Who Laughs suggested "Tejas", the Caddo word for "friend." So it was decided, and we indeed had more friends in Texas.

––––––––––

When we arrived at the east bank of the Trinity, we found it too deep to ford. The land here was swampy and plagued with mosquitoes. It wouldn't be a healthy place to wait until the river dropped. It was here that Rob returned to his old self. He recommended we build a ferry to float the wagons across one at a time.

Chopping down several tall straight pine trees, we trimmed,

peeled and cut them into thirty foot lengths. We beveled the ends of the logs across the bottom end before we placed them side by side. Each log was notched to accept the rounded half of a split log. The split logs were placed flat side up and fastened with black locust pegs. The ferry was about ten feet wide. We used a triple team of six mules to haul the raft into the shallow water as far as they could go.

Rob took a harnessed mare and fastened a light rope to the hames of her harness. He led the mare into the water until she had to swim. At that point, he held on to the harness and let her find her way across. The rope she was towing had been fastened to a stout two inch manila rope which followed in their wake. Once she had reached solid footing on the other side, he reeled in the lighter rope and fastened the larger rope to a large stout tree. Yelling instructions back to us, he had us fasten our end also, so that the rope cleared the surface of the water by a few feet.

"I need another harnessed mare and two inch rope over here." Lucius volunteered. He was thirteen and old enough to be some help. His only concession to his mother was a safety rope that tied him to the harness if he should lose his grip. I also told him how to quickly untie it if the horse floundered in the flood waters. The east end of his rope was fastened to the front of the ferry. As he swam across, I could see the pride mixed with anxiety in Nancy's eyes. Once across, this rope was fastened between the two horses, and connected back to the front of the raft. Rob had us use lighter rope to tie the front and back of the raft to the large cable above the water on the up stream side. It was only then that I realized that it was to stop the current from carrying the raft down river.

"Before you load the first wagon, fasten another two inch

rope to the back of the raft and make it fast to something in case things go wrong. If it works right, you can hitch it to a couple of horses and haul the ferry back to you." He sure made it sound easy.

"Now put my wagon on first. If this doesn't work, I don't want anybody else getting their stuff wet. Tanner, you still feel like driving it?"

We pushed the raft back through the shallow water until the beveled ends gently touched the edge. Tanner urged the mules onto the strange contraption. They did better than I had expected them to do. Rob laid into the mares across the river who pulled with all their might, but could not budge the loaded ferry. "Aaron, get some men behind the ferry with long stout poles and see if you can pry her loose. Once it starts to move, the mares can take it from there." We did as he asked, and amazingly, the ferry gently broke free and began to move forward. As it did, the line to the opposite bank was drawing tight, and the ferry was soon across. Tanner whipped the mules into leaving their dry spot as they dragged the wagons into the shallow water at the other side.

Seeing how it was done, we hitched the east rope to a team of mules who quickly pulled the empty ferry back. Rob had replaced the two mares with the four mules from his wagon. With the extra pulling power, very little leverage was needed to get the ferry floating. It took us all day, but it was done. Rob was a hero. A crude sign was carved and nailed in place on both banks: *Captain Rob's Ferry, 1822. Free to the public.*

We pulled far enough away from the Trinity bottoms to set up camp where the mosquitoes weren't so bad. Although we were all tired, we knew we had conquered a huge obstacle that day. After a big meal, we all slept like babies.

The Trinity behind us, we made it to the Smith farm for our last night's camp before reaching the Navasota. I rode ahead to make sure it would be all right for a group as large as ours to impose on their hospitality. I found the cabin door swinging open and the livestock gone. Easing the stallion around the homestead, I found the decomposing bodies of a man and a woman. Comanche arrows were sticking out of the putrid remains. Dismounting, I found a shovel in the barn and buried the bodies where they lay. I was pretty sure it was Asa and Janie. I drove a piece of broken board into the disturbed ground at the head of both graves and scratched their initials into the wood with my knife. I couldn't find any sign of the children and feared the Comanche had taken them.

My stomach revolted as I remembered better days with the Smiths. I vomited up my breakfast in the edge of their garden. After composing myself, I rode back to get the others. I warned Rob and Nancy what to expect. We pulled the wagons into the weedy homestead, unhitched the livestock and tended them in the corral before turning them out to graze under guard. Once camp was set, I explained things as well as I could to the others.

"These would have been our closest neighbors, Asa and Janie Smith and their two children. I buried Asa and Janie this morning, and don't know what has become of the children. We must never forget for even a minute that this is a dangerous country. The Smiths lived here alone. I hope we will find safety in numbers."

I donned my black frock coat and retrieved my Bible, I read a few verses from Ecclesiastes. We sang a hymn and I led us in a prayer of mercy for the Smiths, for their children if they lived, and for God's mercy on us. It was a solemn congregation.

After the brief funeral service Kassie found me. "Major, what about Nick, Cody and Chance? Isn't their cabin only a few miles from here?" Tears welled up in her eyes.

"Yes, Kassie. It's an easy half day ride to their cabin. Just remember, there are three of them, all good shots, with plenty of extra guns. I can only hope we find them safe tomorrow." I felt a cold hand clamp around my heart. What would we find?

The next morning a quiet somber group hitched their wagons and fell into line as we headed west. By afternoon we would know the fate of our friends. Suddenly, three well mounted men appeared from around a bend in the road. I recognized the horses as our own, and Cody's coonskin cap was unmistakable, even at that distance. I spurred the stud horse into a lope heading straight for them. They didn't recognize my horse, but they soon realized who was riding him. We all broke into a gallop, whooping as we rode.

"Thank God you're alive!"

"Thank God and good shootin' rifles." Chance laughed.

"Kassie with you, Major?" I nodded as Nick headed east at a gallop toward the slowly approaching wagons. Spotting Kassie's wagon, he tied his mare to the tail gate and swept up onto the wagon box beside her.

Cody and Chance eased their horses into a long trot beside me as we headed back to the wagons. Chance filled in the rest of the story. "One night, about two weeks ago, the dogs got to actin' up. We had the stock penned in the stalls, and we checked all our guns. A dozen or so Comanche rode right between the cabins like they owned the place. Some of 'em jumped off their horses making a run for the livestock. The rest of them came a whoopin' for the cabin. We shot six of 'em right off. Guess they didn't know we had extra guns. The dogs got a hold of a couple of 'em who were trying to untie the stall gates. We wounded one of 'em before they got tired of fightin' the dogs. They grabbed up their horses and lit out. One of 'em was carrying a little girl. As they rode by the corner of the other cabin, he bashed that baby's brains out on the logs." Chance stopped talking and seemed to be collecting himself. "I shot that Indian myself. Another had a little boy up behind him on his horse. That kid was screamin' bloody murder. Cody opened the cabin door and shot that Comanche right through the head at fifty feet. The boy is okay. All he will tell us is that his name is Will. I think he is the Smiths' boy. He holds on to Cody like he's his daddy. We buried the little girl, but don't know her name. It was pretty bad, Major."

We had arrived in our land of destiny. But Texas had shown us her untamed side. Clawing a life from our home on the Camino Real would be a tempestuous struggle. We had come far from our picnics by the mill pond.

# 14

## April 1822, Navasota Crossing, Camino Real, Texas

CODY, NICK AND CHANCE had done more than we expected. They had finished two other cabins, essentially identical to the first two. They were placed to form the other corners of our "fort."

"Where did you muleskinners learn to build like that? Those cabins look almost respectable," I said with a sparkle in my eyes.

"Oh, Major. I reckon you taught us about as good as a preacher could" Nick laughed. He had not turned loose of Kassie since he had met her on the road. We decided the northwest cabin would belong to them. Kassie was sweeping it out and setting up her things quick as a flash. For now, Cody and Chance would share it with them. And where Cody went, Will was never far.

Richard Moore, our blacksmith, and his family were given the northeast cabin. They had also "inherited" Gray Jamison. He and the Moore's son, Tanner, had become fast friends.

The southeastern corner cabin was assigned to the Joe Morgan family. He was a carpenter by trade and a fine farmer, too. His wife, daughter, and son, Logan, settled in to the cabin with him.

The original cabin in the southwest corner had been pre-determined to be ours. Nancy was pleased with it. "Aaron, it is bigger and better than I expected. With the other families living here, I feel safer, too."

I gave her a big hug and carried her over the threshold of our cabin. There was much of the hard side of Texas Nancy had not seen yet; perhaps she never would. But, like she said, there was safety in numbers. Rob had decided to stay on here until he got a ferry built on the Navasota. It could be forded much of the year, but when the rains came, it would prove very useful. He decided to delay moving on to the Brazos for a while. He eventually planned to settle there and build a ferry and steam boat landing. The other families that had traveled with us pushed on farther west to their claims on the Colorado River.

Chance rode with me to show off the rest of the place with the improvements. They had built a rail fence around the perimeter of the pasture surrounding the fort. Beyond that to the north, they had cleared, plowed and planted ten acres of oats, which were already knee high. They had thrown up a fence around the grain field to keep the wild cattle and horses out. Inside the fort, they had built a large store-house, corn cribs, and a smoke house. Although there was much yet to do, we had a good beginning.

We built a cabin much like the others along the north

side, connecting it to the other cabins with palisades. The space between the cabins on the north wall was made into extra stalls. This cabin was for Chance, Cody and little Will. It gave Nick and Kassie some space of their own. We built a palisade south from the Moores' cabin until it connected with the Morgan's cabin. This gave us an east wall with stalls and storage on the inside. Finally, a solid gate assembly was built between the front two cabins out of heavy sawn timbers. The gate was tied into the Morgan's cabin on the southeast corner and ours on the southwest corner with palisades, also. The perimeter of the fort was now enclosed.

Each evening after supper the women and children were given lessons in loading guns until they could do it with their eyes closed. All of the women and older children were taught to use them as well. Even the younger children were taught to fire a shotgun. A small hunting party of Comanche would give the fort a wide berth. However, we might look tempting to a larger war band.

Every day we turned the stock out to graze during the day, always under close supervision. There was a fenced pasture of roughly ten acres surrounding the fort where the animals could be kept during times of increased danger, so they could be quickly brought into the fort. Every night the saddle horses, stallion, mules, jack, bull and milk cows were penned in the stalls within the fort. They were too valuable to risk losing to predators, raiders or straying. The others could be replaced, but these could not.

The jack had been turned in with our best mares. We hoped to raise some top quality mules. They were so scarce in Texas they commanded a fine price. We had the Thoroughbred stallion running with the best of the native mares. We hoped to add some height, length and weight to their offspring, while retaining the quickness and toughness of the little native mares.

Whenever the opportunity presented, we would capture longhorn heifers and try to gentle them somewhat before turning them in with our Shorthorn bull and two Shorthorn milk cows. These prize cattle were seldom out of sight and usually pastured near the fort.

The hogs had to be kept away from the fort in an enclosure near the cultivated land to the north to minimize the odor. Their pen was built to be both bear and panther proof. If Indians tried to steal the hogs, we would be too far away to stop them. But a hog could prove a very difficult thing to steal. The chickens wandered wherever they wanted to go, but their laying boxes were placed along the back walls of the stalls.

Fresh sweet milk, butter and buttermilk were kept in crocks lowered into the cool water of the well.

We all pitched in to build the blacksmith and carpenter shops. They were both built on the south side of the road facing the fort. The shops weren't even finished when travelers began to stop for their services.

Rob now decided it was time to start on a ferry here on the Navasota before building one on the much more difficult Brazos. The crossing here on the Navasota was usually shallow enough to ford, but heavy rains and the steep banks could quickly make the usually tame river very deep and swift. He used the same pattern he had used on the Trinity with one important modification. Here he used a large block and tackle to be able to work the ferry from the east bank. He charged a little for folks who chose to use it. If he was gone, one of the older boys would take care of it for half the collected fare.

We set about enlarging our cultivated field by another fifteen acres. We planted ten acres to corn, and the balance to potatoes and vegetables. The soil was rich deep loam. We harvested our first crop at Navasota Crossing when we cut and threshed the oats. The grain was cleaned and stored for the winter and the straw was placed in the lofts.

Our friends, the Tonkawa, Waco and Wichita came to trade and to make use of our carpenter and smith. Joe Morgan and his son, Logan, began selecting trees to saw for lumber. The logs were stacked behind their shop to season.

As the summer progressed, our crops grew beautifully in the rich dark soil and enjoyed just the right amount of rain. Nancy picked a good place for her orchard. She had set out several peach, apple, apricot, pear, plum and cherry trees soon after we arrived. They were thriving in their new environment and should produce some fruit by the third summer. We built a special rail fence about six feet high to keep the deer out.

We would shoot a wild longhorn as often as we needed fresh beef. Anything we didn't eat then was dried for jerky. We kept the hides, as you could make almost anything with rawhide. Nick and Cody were able to capture several wild horses that they broke for riding. The wild stallions were killed and the mares added to the herd.

There was a small salt spring a couple of miles south of the settlement. We would fill shallow pans with brine. When the water had evaporated we scrapped the salt into small sacks. There was enough for all our needs and a little to trade.

A little hard work put another fifteen acres to the plow. It was too late to plant summer crops, but we planted oats and wheat plus a few acres of winter vegetables. The rabbits and coons kept raiding the cabbage patch. The boys were kept busy shooting them and chasing them away. The rabbits were pretty good groceries, but I didn't care for the coons. Kassie would roast a coon with sweet potatoes that Nick and Cody enjoyed, but the rest of us declined. We got the corn in the crib, the fodder in the loft, and the vegetables in the cellars. We needed to make a trip to Natchitoches for supplies before the Comanche raiding parties began to roam during the time of the Comanche Moon in October and November.

———————

We had a wagon load of cowhides, pelts, and several sacks of jerky to take to Natchitoches for trade, plus a stack of letters to post. Chance and Rob rode beside the wagon as I drove east on the Camino Real. We needed some supplies for our settlement before winter. But our urgency was not just supplies. We needed to be back before the first full moon in October, the Comanche Moon. It was then that our fiercest enemies went on their annual raids. They were a threat year round, but that period of time each fall was dedicated to violence. With our lightly loaded wagon pulled by our four best mules, we were able to make twenty miles a day. We reached the ferry on the Trinity by dusk the first day and crossed before dark. The cool fall weather had eliminated the mosquito problems, but we had no desire to tarry in the unsafe and unhealthy Trinity bottoms. We carried grain for the livestock as there would not be time for them to graze much. Two hard days put us at the Campos farm near Nacogdoches. We found them well and pushed on the next morning. Two more long days brought us to the campsite on the west bank of the Sabine. It was just fully dark and too late to risk crossing. We forded the river back into the United States just before sun rise the next morning and were in Natchitoches by sunset.

Louis bon Chance was smoking his pipe on his porch as we pulled up. "Hello, Papa! What's for supper?" Chance laughed.

"Son, I hoped you would show up here soon. You know, Chance, you were born hungry and never did fill up."

We spent a good evening catching up on news. Louis made us a fair trade for our goods, and we spent the next day loading the wagon for the return trip.

"Let me see, Major. That's twenty pounds of coffee beans, ten pounds of sugar, one small keg and ten horns of good gunpowder, lead shot, a keg of nails, a sack of seed wheat and vegetable seeds, four bolts of cloth, some tobacco, and a crate of house wares. What else do you want?"

"Louis, your memory is shorter than your nose. The mill, the mill."

"Oh, oui. It has rollers to press cane for syrup, and stones for grinding grain. Ha! I know what you forgot. The seed for the ribbon cane, you know, the sweet sorghum. You can't make syrup without that. I already put it in the wagon." It was his turn to laugh at me.

Rob had wandered down to the steamboat landing. The current had swept whatever had remained of the *Samuel Brown* downstream. I walked down to stand by him. His eyes glistened. "It was my fault. I was in charge. It was my fault."

"Rob, how many times have you known of a steam engine to explode? You kept it serviced, you didn't abuse it, you weren't pushing too much steam, the engine was barely turning. These things happen. It wasn't your fault. Come on, the wagon is loaded and supper is almost ready. Tomorrow we head back to Texas."

I turned to go, but he lingered a while, throwing stones in the murky water of the Red River. He came back to Louis' store in time for supper. Louis had some mail for us he had forgotten to give us on our arrival. There was a letter from Charles Contois sending his regards and asking about us. I wrote a reply on the back of his letter and left it with Louis to send. Rob had a letter from some of his family. He didn't send a response. The last letter was from my brother James in South Carolina. He had sent it to Charles and asked him to forward it to me.

Dear Brother,

I have sad news. Father fell and broke his hip on the ice in February. He took pneumonia and died a month later. Our dear mother was so shaken by his loss that she died in her sleep soon after. I wish there was some way to get the news to you sooner, but even if there had been, you would not have been able to have returned before they died. Father's will left the plantation to me as the eldest. We have moved into their cabin to better oversee the work. To each of the rest of you he left $500. I have sent it to you by way of a letter of credit on our bank in New Orleans. They have been instructed to send coin to Natchitoches for you in care of Louis bon Chance. We pray that you and your family are safe and well. Father asked me before he died to send you his gold watch from London. It had belonged to our grandfather, Thomas Turner, Senior. Father was very proud of it and insisted that you have it. You will find it enclosed with your money. We buried them by Thomas and Priscella in the little cemetery on the

Harrington Plantation. We hope to hear from you.

Your brother,

James

When I had last left South Carolina with Nancy and the children, it never occurred to me that I would not see my parents again. A sense of sadness came over me.

My grandfather had carved a home out of the South Carolina wilderness. He, my father and uncles had fought the British to secure our freedom. The blood stained red soils of South Carolina had nourished and sustained my family to the fourth generation. I knew now I was unlikely to ever see it again. With both my parents dead, I doubted I would ever make the trip back up the Pee Dee River to see my brothers and sisters again.

But my home, family and life was now in Texas. I knew I was not likely to ever return to the Carolinas. I wrote James a letter outlining our life and experiences in Texas on the Camino Real at Navasota Crossing.

Rob stood beside me as I read by the fireplace. "I see my dark mood has passed to you, Major. I'm sorry about your parents."

"What was your news?"

"Oh, there are lawsuits waiting for me in New Orleans because of the explosion. I think I'll be staying in Texas for a while."

"So will I, my friend. So will I."

The horses and mules had rested enough to make good time heading west. The roads were dry, and the weather was cool and crisp as we retraced our steps to Navasota Crossing. We pulled up at the fort just after dark as a bright half moon rose in the east. We were only a week from the Comanche Moon.

# 15

October 1822, Navasota Crossing, Texas

SOMETHING ABOUT THE way the dogs were barking brought me sitting bolt upright in bed fully awake. It was a good half hour before dawn. There was a chill in the cabin air as the fire was down to embers. The barking wasn't like the alarm they gave for a bear or a bobcat. There was urgency in their tone. I quietly awakened the family, cautioning them to remain silent. Rob, Lucius, Louise, Marcus and Nancy had gotten up quietly and quickly, taking the guns from the pegs above the rifle ports and priming the pans. I gave a sharp yank on the rawhide cord that ran from our cabin north to Nick's cabin and another that ran east to the Morgan's cabin. Each was attached to a small bell to alert our companions of danger. They had similar cords connecting to the other cabins. The replying ring indicated they had heard.

The wooden blocks closing the rifle ports were

carefully eased out. A single candle had been lit to provide just enough light to handle the guns. A tiny twinkle of light could be seen through the rifle ports of the other cabins. Our neighbors were on the alert, too. As the sky lightened slowly, I could make out the silhouettes of small groups of deer south and west of the fort. At this quiet hour they should be grazing peacefully, but they kept looking back toward the timber along the river. Something was making them nervous.

As the first glimmer of sunlight broke in the eastern sky, I saw a metallic reflection in the woods to the west. With a sudden bound, the deer bolted away from their natural cover along the river and ran to the south. Those who had disturbed the peace slowly materialized from the timber to the west.

"Rob, recognize the war paint and markings on those horses?"

"Sure do, Major. Looks like we got some genuine Comanche company for breakfast."

I saw Nancy shudder and the kids glance at me. "Comanche, Papa?" Lucius asked.

"Yes, son. I'm afraid so."

As we spoke, their war band eased out of the woods and began a slow deliberate ride around the fields surrounding the fort. They disappeared from our sight, but I assumed the other cabins could see them. There were twenty-five or thirty of them. They were at the extreme range of common frontier smoothbore muskets, but our rifles were deadly accurate at that range. We held our fire. Maybe the five cabins with palisades would deter them. There were seventeen adults and children old enough to handle a gun. But our fire power was not evenly distributed. There were six in our cabin, and only two in the Teel's.

The Comanche leader rode a few yards farther out of the woods. Standing in his stirrups, he yelled and shook his lance against us. Plunging it into the ground, he let out a blood-curdling war cry. The whole band began to circle again. When they reached the road, they turned, charging north along the lane straight at our gate. Arrows filled the air, striking around our rifle ports. We were able to bring three guns to bear on them, as could the Morgans. At thirty yards we fired at the galloping riders. We heard three shots from the Morgans' cabin, too. Two Comanche had been knocked from their horses either dead or wounded. Grabbing already loaded rifles, we were able to fire a hurried second volley just as they hit the gate. One more slumped off his horse. We would be in bad shape if they were able to breech the gate.

"Rob, Lucius, Marcus! Grab those shotguns and pistols and follow me. Nancy, you and Louisa bar the door and stand by with your shotguns!"

The four of us ran to the gate to see three Indians already at the top of the palisade. Our buckshot at fifteen feet killed them all. We made for the gate, firing through the gun ports on either side of it. Our second barrels dropped four more. The Comanche had run rawhide ropes through the gate and were pulling it down with their horses. The bar on the gate was holding, but the hinges were pulling loose. Rob and I slashed the ropes as lances flashed through the gun ports.

I heard Marcus scream in pain as a lance sliced into his left arm. With his right hand, he raised the .69 caliber pistol and unleashed its deadly load of buck and ball into his attacker's face at point blank range splattering Marcus with gore. As we drove them back from the gate, the guns from the cabins fired, killing three more.

The Comanche retreated to the road. It appeared sixteen of their number lay dead or wounded on the lane and around the gate. They regrouped, their painted horses prancing in the sunlight. Slowly, their leader rode to the mouth of the lane with his bow held high above his head. He shouted at us in Comanche. I responded in Spanish.

"I, Pony Who Runs, will leave if you allow us to retrieve our dead and wounded. If you do not, we will return with more warriors and burn your log houses."

I answered, fury in my voice. "If we allow you to do this, you must not return this year to attack us. Only send four men leading their horses to collect your dead and injured. We will not harm you unless you deceive us."

"I, Pony Who Runs, give you my word. These warriors obey me. I give no promise for next year."

"It is agreed."

Four men moved forward leading their horses, their bows slung over their saddles. They draped the bodies over the nervous horses and loaded the wounded on travois behind the horses. Pony Who Runs called out. "We leave now, and will not return this year. Know that I only speak for my own war band and no other." Turning in the morning sunlight, they disappeared into the timber.

My mouth was parched and my hands shaking. I ran to check on Marcus. The wound was clean and bleeding freely. Nancy cleaned and bandaged his injured arm. Slowly our neighbors began to appear from their cabins clutching loaded weapons. Several of the women and children were crying. Will, the lone survivor from the Smith family shook his fists in anger. "They killed Mama, they killed Papa. I hate them injuns!" These were the first words he had spoken in a year. He turned and ran to Cody who picked him up and held him tightly.

"Guess he can talk after all, Major."

"I want all the men over here now. The rest of you load every gun we got, and keep a sharp watch out the rifle ports. Fellas, we got lucky. We came darn close to having Comanche loose in here. If this ever happens again, I'm sending Rob and Lucius from our cabin to the gate. Everybody else just stay put like you were. If everyone runs for the gate, then we got a hole somewhere else."

Joe Morgan spoke up. "Major, we've got a blind spot right in front of the gate. If we move the gate back even with the peak of our cabin roofs, we could cut rifle ports in the end of the cabin and be able to cover the gate. We can leave the one we've got standing until the new one is built."

"Joe, you sound like an old Indian fighter. Let's do it."

"Thank God the dogs woke us up," Nick added.

"Major, maybe during the time of the Comanche moon we ought to take turns leaving two men on guard," Chance suggested.

Rob joined in the discussion. "I think Chance is right. And what if they tossed torches on the roof? I'd like to see us make some gutters to catch rain water in big barrels along each wall, and keep a couple of buckets by each one. We might put a torch out before it ever started a fire. And I sure wish there was more of us living here. The fort is getting kind of full of cabins, but if more folks move near here, they could head to the fort if there was trouble."

We started building new stronger gates that very day. Gutters were made of tree bark until something better could be found, and the barrels were filled with well water. Two buckets were hung by every barrel. We started sharing guard duty that night. We were learning from experience.

Until the next full moon, the Hunter's Moon, we kept guard over the livestock in the pastures all day. All our changes had been put in place, and the new improved gate was hung. It did seem safer. I felt Nancy tremble at night next to me in bed as she whispered, "We'll be okay, Aaron."

Marcus' arm healed well, but the scar on his arm was small compared to the one left on his spirit. He cried out in his sleep from nightmares and was withdrawn during the day. "Papa, I'm all tore up inside. That Comanche could have killed me if I hadn't jumped. And I saw him. I saw his face was gone when I shot him. I see his face at night." Hot tears streamed down his face.

"Marcus, you did what you had to do to stay alive and protect your family. We didn't come here looking for trouble, but those Comanche sure as heck did. They came here to kill us. We had no choice but to fight. You just did what you had to do. You were real brave."

"I don't feel very brave, I just feel sick inside."

At a loss for words of comfort or wisdom, I just held him until he had cried it all out. "I'm proud of you Marcus. I'm proud to call you my son." We never spoke of it again.

# 16

March 1823, Navasota Crossing, Texas

WE SPENT THE BALANCE of the winter enlarging the plowed fields. The various ownership tracts were staked out and marked with piles of stones. But for now we held our cropland and pastures in common. We hunted wild cattle for their hides and meat. Many times we ate beef three times a day, but all the excess we made into jerky for the winter months and to sell or trade. We roped heifers to add to our growing herds. We also spent profitable time catching wild horses. Nick and Cody could break them to ride in about six weeks. They were plentiful in Texas and did not sell as well as our crossbred horses and mules, but there was a pretty good market in Louisiana. They would drive a herd to Natchitoches once or twice a year.

We fenced along the flood line of the Navasota to keep the cattle out of the river bottoms. We made another fence along Boggy Creek as it angled away to the northeast. At the point where the creek emerged from the forest to the east, we built a rail fence running roughly southward until it intersected the road. Finally, we ran a perimeter fence along the road all the way back to the settlement. We had about twelve square miles fenced together in a block. This would help keep the wild horses and cattle off our land and our tame animals contained.

The early gardens were planted to peas, carrots, cabbage, onions and a variety of greens. We enjoyed the change in our diet, as beef, beans and corn bread could get a little tiresome in the winter months. We had quickly learned to love the native pecans which grew in profusion along the river. The nuts were a very welcome addition to our diet. As the spring warmed, we planted corn, beans and peas, sweet potatoes, squash and melons. We also planted a few acres to sweet sorghum for syrup and a few acres to tobacco.

By late spring there was a trickle of settlers heading west on the Camino Real into parts of Austin's Colony farther west. Many of them admired what we had accomplished here. We were happy to let them camp on the unfenced pastures south of the road and graze their stock on the good grass there. They usually had plenty of supplies, as they hadn't been too long on the trail. However, they often needed the services of our carpenter and blacksmith. The spring had been wet, and the river was often up. Rob was making a good little bit of money with his ferry. Occasionally someone would carry packets of mail from the east. There was a letter from Joseph Hawkins inquiring of our well being, and to let us know to expect a flood of settlers by summer. He had taken the liberty of arranging for a load of trade goods to arrive soon to stock a trading post.

We built a store on the south side of the road. It carried a few bolts of cloth, some kitchen and house wares, musket flints, powder and shot. We had sides of bacon, jerky, dried beans and peas for sale along with small sacks of salt, coffee and piloncillos of sugar. We also sold limited amounts of honey and sacks of pecans in the shell. We took a variety of things in for trade, especially hides and pelts. Our hams, eggs, dairy products and syrup were too precious to trade.

Four families decided to stake their claims at Navasota Crossing. The Painter family of four was the first. Mr. Painter was a worker of clay making pottery, tile, and bricks. He found the red clay south along the river to be exactly what he wanted. They built a cabin near the deposits of clay and built kilns for firing his works. A family named Lane chose to stay, too. He was a tanner by trade, using his finished leather to build harness, tack and saddles. Cow hides were plentiful here. He brought a wife and three strong sons with him. They established their tannery south of the road near the Painter's cabin. The Lanes dug pits for curing the hides and a hide shed in addition to their large cabin. A cobbler and his family named Black settled here, too. Mr. Black could make and mend shoes and boots, and he knew how to do minor repairs on many things. His wife was a seamstress. Travelers were asking for his services even as he was building his cabin next to our store. Finally, the Willis family decided to stay. He was a wheelwright and cooper. He saw the need for repairing wagons and wheels and barrels. He was as busy as our blacksmith and carpenter. He built his shop and cabin on the south side of the road next to the Black's cabin. We had added thirteen people old enough to handle a gun to our community, plus ten children. In times of danger, there would be thirty of us defending the fort. The additional children brought extra joy to our lives.

Nancy approached me with an idea. "Aaron, you know that I was a school teacher in Georgia. We have enough children here to need a school. Would you build a school for me? We could make it big enough to use as a meeting hall and church on Sundays."

How could I say no to this wonderful woman, the love of my life? She gave so much of herself and asked so little in return. Even now she was asking for the benefit of others. "Of course I will. I assume you will be the teacher?"

She smiled and handed me a sketch of the school.

As Joseph Hawkins had predicted, the road was crowded with wagons heading west on the Camino Real. Chance took a wagon back to Natchitoches for more supplies for the store, leading a string of horses behind the wagon. He had sold all the horses before he reached the Sabine. Our Caddo, Wichita and Tonkawa friends visited occasionally, too. They were amazed at the growth of our community and the number of wagons on the road. They often left orders for things they wanted at the store.

Rob's ferry was busy all day every day. He left Tanner Lane to run the ferry while he went on to the Brazos to establish a ferry there. He convinced Blake and Tyler Lane to go with him to build it. He had shipped in an abundance of ropes, cables, blocks and tackles. They built two ferries and a cabin on the east bank. The Lane brothers were so impressed with the Brazos bottom lands, they decided to take up their claims there. They added another cabin and stockade to protect their livestock. They were now our newest neighbors, a day's ride away. They realized they would be very vulnerable there during raiding season. Rob decided that during the Comanche Moon, they would board up their cabins, beach their ferries, and move all their livestock back to Navasota Crossing. In time, their community there would grow to where it could defend itself.

The summer rains were all we could have expected. The crops did well. By fall our corn cribs were bulging, the smoke houses filled, and the lofts full of winter fodder. We had crates of potatoes, sweet potatoes, pumpkins and cabbage in the various cellars. Dried beans and peas were sacked in the store houses. We had planted five acres of sweet sorghum to press for syrup to make sorghum molasses. The freshly pressed juice was slowly simmered in large shallow pans until it reached the right thickness. Our mill was turned by a mule harnessed to the end of a long pole. As the mule walked in monotonous circles, the mill turned relentlessly. The steel rollers squeezed out the sweet juice, while the stone rollers were used to grind corn meal and the precious little amount of wheat into flour. We had enough corn that we filled many barrels with corn meal. So far, 1823 had been kind to us. Our roots were spreading deep down into the rich Texas soil.

# 17

## Spring 1824, Navasota Crossing, Texas

NAVASOTA CROSSING wintered well. The Comanche were preoccupied fighting the settlers along the Colorado and had not come this far to the east. The folks on the Colorado had a pretty tough winter because of the incessant Comanche raiding. We had begun to have religious services in our log school building on Sundays. For the sake of safety, men were on guard at the ferry, the fort and with the livestock during services. There was no room in the small fort for the combined school and church building All the adults, both men and women, carried weapons to church as did the older children. Such a scene would seem out of place in the United States, but here it was every day life. There was never a shortage of volunteers for guard duty during church. I suspected it reflected on my preaching. I wasn't the best preacher in Texas, but right now I was almost the only one.

After services on Sunday, Tanner Moore walked up sheepishly to me and tugged on my coat sleeve. I looked at the fair-haired, blue-eyed boy expecting some question about God's word.

"Reverend, I want you to have this." He extended his hand and placed a small wedge of silver in my hand.

"Tanner, we already took up the offering. Do you want me to add this to it?"

"No, sir. It's for you. I reckon you must need it. Pa says you are the poorest preacher he ever heard." With a giggle, he ran away with Logan and Gray close behind. I had been set up, and Cody Teel was laughing the hardest.

"Thanks for the two bits, Owl Killer. Hope it wasn't all you had left!" The joke had been at my expense, and we all had a good laugh.

---

As the spring arrived, we had some of our first successes with our livestock program. My beautiful Thoroughbred stallion had sired a large number of foals on the native mares. They were long and muscular, with an obvious look of quality to them. Our Spanish jack had fathered a nice crop of mule foals from our draft mares. They were big, strong and mostly bay. Our Shorthorn bull passed thickness and muscle mass to his calves from the longhorn heifers. Almost as important, they were much more gentle than their wild cousins. The crossbred cattle were an assortment of colors, spots and stripes, but obviously superior to the longhorns.

Our flocks of chicken had grown enough that we could

have eggs every day for breakfast, and the young cockerels sure were tasty fried on Sundays. We had enough hogs now that we could eat bacon whenever we wanted it, and we had ham and loin meat for special occasions. These things, taken for granted in settled places, were luxuries here and a sign that we were becoming established as a community.

---

In the late winter, Nick and Cody helped the boys each start a two year old horse. Lucius and Marcus had crossbreed fillies from our herd. Cody gave Logan and Gray each a young mustang gelding. Tanner Moore had the pretty little filly he had traded from the Indians.

Each day when their chores and school work were finished, the boys would lead their horses to the corral the Teel brothers used to train livestock. Cody and Nick showed them how to get their horses used to new things like blankets and saddles. They would flop and flap a saddle blanket around one of the young horses, then throw the blanket down on the ground in front of its head. The curious animal would sniff the blanket until it was convinced it wasn't a predator. Then the blanket got gently dragged over the horse's head, down it neck, back and legs. Once the horse was used to the blanket, the boys would put the blanket on the colt's back and lead him around wearing it. They repeated the process with the saddle. Of course, a saddle rattles and clatters more than a blanket, and the conditioning process took a little longer. Once they were no longer scared of the saddle, it would be cinched loosely into place and the horse led until he quieted. Soon, both the front and back cinch were fastened. Then the cinches were firmly tightened.

Once this was accomplished, Nick or Cody would gently step up into the left stirrup and climb down. After repeating this step several times, they would quietly swing their right leg across the saddle so that they were astride the horse. If they were going to encounter problems, this would be the place. But the younger boys had done a good job of gentling their horses and not a single horse bucked. At this point, the boys took over the process, and once seated on the horse either Nick or Cody would lead them around the corral.

Once both the horse and rider seemed comfortable, they would be handed a set of reins attached to the sides of the halters to use while being led. At some point, the lead rope would be quietly removed and each boy was guiding his own horse. This continued in the corral until the horses had some idea of what it meant to turn and stop with rein pressure. The horses wouldn't be introduced to a bits or spurs until much later in their education.

They began to take daily rides outside the corral following Nick on his horse, with Cody and his horse bringing up the rear. There were a few minor spills from jittery horses and inexperienced riders, but nothing worse than bumps and bruises.

On the fifth day of riding out of the corral things changed. As the seven horses and riders passed through the dried prairie grass north of the fort, Tanner's horse disturbed a hen who was foraging for bugs. The startled hen burst into clumsy flight, squawking like she was being killed right under the little filly. As the chicken erupted from the tall grass to escape, a dozen or more sister hens exploded into confused chaos all around the horses.

The panicked horses rolled their eyes and squealed in terror. They began to buck for all they were worth. First one horse and then the others broke into a head long gallop to the north to escape what ever dreadful beast was trying to eat them. The Teel brother managed to get in front of the stampeding young horses and riders, but they blazed right on by them like the devil had them by the tail.

The rail fence around the oat field stretched across their escape route. The filly Lucius was riding managed to clear the four foot rails, but dumped him in the dirt on the other side of the fence with the reins still in his hands. Marcus' filly swerved at the last minute rather than attempt to jump the fence. Marcus was thrown unceremoniously into the fence as the little horse ran away. The galloping of their horses had unseated both Tanner and Gray in the turnip patch. Tanner had the wind knocked out of him, and Gray ate a mouthful of dirt, but neither was hurt.

Logan's mustang galloped around the fence until he had a straight shot at freedom. He increased his speed to a dead run as Logan held on the mane and saddle horn for dear life. The creek loomed ominously ahead. It was deep, wide and cold at this time of the year. Seeing the obstacle, the little mustang gathered all his remaining strength for a mighty bound to jump across the creek. He jumped high and he jumped long, but he didn't jump far enough. Both horse and rider disappeared under the water. First a hat bobbed to the surface; then the horse appeared and swam to the far bank. While he stood shaking in an attempt to rid himself of both the saddle and the cold water, Logan popped to the surface gasping for air. Nick roped him with his first try and dragged the soaked boy to the bank. Cody rode down the creek a way where there was an easy place to splash across and caught the tired horse. Nick set Logan on the back of his saddle and headed back to the corrals while Cody led the mustang.

The other boys had managed to catch their horses and had them back at the corral. The story of the great runaway stampede made for good story telling for many years, and it was the general consensus that Logan needed a bath anyway.

———

On a warm afternoon in the late spring of 1824, Logan Morgan, Tanner Moore, Gray Jamison and a handful of the other boys had gone swimming at a good place on the river near the tannery. They had decided the water was too cold to enjoy, so they had gotten out and were putting on their clothes. As a prank, Logan threw Gray's shoes into the shallow water near the bank. Gray waded in to try to find them when Logan yelled, "Indians!"

Gray thought it was another prank and kept looking for his shoes. "Y'all shut up and help me find my shoes!"

Logan screamed, "Run, Gray, run!"

Gray looked up to see three canoes filled with huge, naked, tattooed Karankawa Indians glide into the shallow water. Two canoes blocked his escape to the river bank. Two braves leapt from the third canoe. Gray was roughly knocked unconscious with a war club and thrown into the canoe. The war canoes turned with the current and rapidly disappeared down stream.

The terrified boys ran through the woods to Mr. Lane's tannery and began to ring the alarm bell to summon help. The Lanes hurried the boys into their cabin and barred the door. The Lanes and their youngest son, Tanner, passed extra guns to the scared boys. They all took up positions at the rifle ports. The Painters had also heard the alarm and abandoned their kilns and took cover in their cabin. With both cabins on alert and armed, they would be able to support each other in the event of an attack. At the Lane's, Logan breathlessly tried to relate what had happened. "Three canoes. Six Indians, big. Hit Gray's head. We ran." He shook all over as he panted.

Hearing the alarm bell, Cody, Chance and I grabbed our horses and galloped to the two southern cabins. Everyone else old enough to hold a gun armed themselves as the gates closed behind us. On hearing the boys' story, we moved all the settlers and valuable livestock inside the fort. We were convinced they were Karankawa.

"Rob, you are in charge here. Chance, Cody, Richard, Joe and Lucius you come with me. Cody, get your dogs. Rob, keep a double guard set. Nobody is allowed outside the fort until we get back."

We saddled up our smaller native horses with our guns, a little food and a canteen of water. Following the river would slow us due to the heavy timber. We would make better time on the prairie that paralleled the river. We headed south at a good trot. We didn't want to ride past them.

About an hour before dark the southwest breeze brought the distinct smell of wood smoke. We had to be close. Chance and Cody took off to scout on foot. We muzzled the dogs and picketed the horses. We kept our guns ready.

An hour later, Cody reappeared from the woods. "We found Gray with a dozen Karankawa. He's okay Mr. Moore. Them Injuns are drunk on something. We gotta hurry. Chance thinks they aim to eat him."

We struck out at a trot following Cody. Here was an eighteen year old leading a group of adults. I guess he had become an adult and I hadn't even noticed. We had smeared ourselves with Chance's stinking mosquito salve, and made sure nothing rattled in our pockets or sloshed in the canteens. He led us to a strip of ground beside the river where no vegetation grew. We could move quietly and swiftly. Within minutes we had found Chance. He used hands signals to stop us and guide us into position. We were close enough to smell them. It was a good thing they were so drunk. Chance indicated that we were each to pick one target and fire on his signal. The quiet night air and the fireflies gave a false sense of peace to the night. We could hear Gray quietly sobbing, so we knew he was still alive.

One of the Karankawa strode over to Gray and back-handed him across the face. As he struck him, Chance shot the tall Indian through the head. Each of us shot and killed our target. I was able to drop a second brave with the other barrel of the Manton. Then we each grabbed shotguns. The buckshot did its job, and the Indians lay dead.

Richard Moore, who had become Gray's guardian, ran to him and cut the bonds around his hands and feet. We laid him near the fire that had been intended to end his life and checked his injuries. He was badly bruised and had a huge swollen lump on the side of his head. Richard gave us his guns and he shifted Gray onto his back for the trip to the horses. We set out at a fast walk and were soon at the edge of the woods in sight of the horses. We handed Gray up to Richard, who had already mounted his horse, setting him behind the saddle and tying him in place. We watered the horses, untied the dogs and set off at an easy trot back to the fort.

It took a couple of days for Gray to feel like getting up and around, but he recovered. Logan had found Gray's shoes and rubbed them down with fresh tallow to keep the leather from shrinking. Gray was only thirteen, but he had seen more horror than most people would see in a life time. The memories of that night, and the explosion that had killed his whole family, haunted his dreams for many years.

———————————

When our spring shipment of goods arrived from New Orleans and Natchitoches, there was a letter from Charles. He told us that our friend Joseph Hawkins had died. He explained the situation in Mexico. Everything was in turmoil. Iturbide had dissolved the legislature and declared himself Emperor of Mexico with full dictatorial powers. A bloodless coup had sent him into exile, and attempts were being made to form a new government under our old friend Santa Anna.

That summer brought a flood of immigrants to the Camino Real. We had expected the influx and had placed ourselves in a position to assist them while turning a modest profit at the same time. We did a brisk business in horses, breeding cattle and mules. We sold hundreds of pounds of jerky, corn, corn meal, salt pork, dried beans and peas. Our craftsmen found plenty of work with repairs and sales of replacement goods. Rob's ferry on the Navasota, as well as the one on the Brazos, did a booming business. We were settled in and finding success.

# 18

January 1825, Navasota Crossing, Texas


THE FALL OF 1824 PASSED in relative peace and prosperity. The Comanche had raided widely, but not east of the Brazos. The Wichita and Tonkawa had banded together to keep their dreaded enemies from coming into their territory. Relations between some of the Anglos had not been good with the Wichita and Tonkawa. By and large, they were peaceful toward the settlers. But their young men were expected to steal a horse to enter full manhood and to be allowed to marry. The settlers believed the theft of livestock was a mortal sin, and launched retaliatory raids to recover livestock. In our district we had a somewhat different approach to dealing with them. Red Wolf of the Tonkawa and Gray Feather of the Waco band of the Wichita had devised a way to maintain peace. When they found their young men had stolen one of our horses, they sent the young man to Navasota Crossing to return the horse that had "strayed." Knowing full well the more likely story, we gladly accepted the returned horse and provided the young man with a reward for its return. Often he would choose a wool blanket, a cooking pot or knife. We knew that his gift would soon find use in the home of a newlywed couple. It kept the peace at little cost to us and maintained the friendship of our allies. We tried never to cheat the Indians in a trade. And we tried to be fair in our barter with them. Peace was a fragile thing that we wanted to preserve.

Stephen Austin established his headquarters in the newly built town of San Felipe on the Colorado. He administered the colony from there with the help of his assistant Samuel Williams, and Austin's brother, Brown.

I had been chosen alcalde at Navasota Crossing. When Austin got established in San Felipe, he made changes to improve the administration of the colony. I was appointed alcalde of the newly appointed Northeast District on Austin's Colony. The district extended a half day's ride north of Navasota Crossing and westward to the Brazos. The district then extended south to the junction of the Navasota River and the Brazos and east to the Trinity. There were no other settlements in the district, but there were several scattered groups of settlers. As alcalde, I was to preside over lawsuits and administer the Colony's law. Appeals could be settled at San Felipe. I was also the military commander of the militia in the district. That job would one day assume more responsibility than I really wanted.

The Mexican Congress, with two representatives from Texas, had adopted the Constitution of 1824. It was modeled on the United States Constitution. It was generally fair and equitable. It retained the racial equality of all men, the supremacy of the

Catholic Church, and the democratic voice of the people. There was a two chambered legislative branch and an independent appointed judiciary. The Constitution reserved most executive rights for the states. This was considered a federal type government versus a centralist or republican form of government. We, the Anglo-Texan settlers who had become Mexican citizens, were able to vote and hold office. We had hoped that Texas might be made an independent state, but the sparse population did not merit that distinction. Instead, we were joined to our neighboring state of Coahuila. Texas would maintain a regional voice at San Antonio, but the capital was Saltillo in Coahuila. We had been allowed to vote on the election of our representatives to the federal legislature, so we had participated in the democratic process. We were happy with the new constitution.

There was a minor sticking point. The constitution prohibited slavery in Mexico. In our whole district there probably weren't any slaves that I could recall. However, on the lower Brazos and Colorado rivers there were some large plantations that owned slaves. Most of the slave owners converted their slaves to indentured servants with very long indentures. This kept the officials happy, but meant nothing to the black men toiling in the sun.

We were all Catholics in name and according to the rolls of the Holy Church. We practiced our own creed of Protestantism in peace and discretion. At Navasota Crossing, our church building had an ornate cross on the wall and beautiful paintings of the Virgin and the Christ. None of us found these objectionable, and they provided enough of an appearance of Catholicism to keep the authorities satisfied.

The Camino Real was our lifeline to the rest of the world.

To the west, we were tied to the Spanish born world of Mexico at San Antonio. To the east, we were still connected by an umbilical cord to our American mother by blood, loyalty and commerce. Through the Camino Real, this vital artery of dust, dirt and mud, flowed the trade of livestock, hides and corn in return for those things we could not supply for ourselves. We lived at the junction of two worlds, of two cultures, two people, and two differing destinies.

Our introduction of Shorthorn blood into the hardy wild longhorn was already producing results. The crosses were bigger, beefier and gentler than the native cattle. Our crossbred stock was in high demand.

Our Spanish jack, when crossed with our draft mares produced spectacular mules. We kept the best for ourselves, and sold the rest as fast as they were broke to plow.

The introduction of our Thoroughbred stallion to the local mares produced unexpectedly fine horses. They were hardy, muscular, quick and tough. They were ideal horses for the environment. We sold them as fast as the Teel brothers could break them.

Nancy, the children and I were happy. We had found our place in the sun, our new home on the frontier. We felt relatively safe and stable. We had put roots deep down in the rich Texas soil. We had accomplished what we had come to do. My dream had become a reality.

But this was Texas, a demanding mistress, still capable of sudden violence. This newly settled territory was far from civilized. The Camino Real connected two widely different worlds that were slowly moving toward an inevitable clash of cultures. The violence of that collision would shake our world to its foundations. Could we survive the coming conflict? Would the land that had seemed our destiny witness our destruction or the fulfillment of our dreams? The Texas winds whispered an unheard prophesy. The streams murmured a warning that we did not comprehend.

# Glossary

Alcalde: roughly the equivalent of an American mayor, but with broader authority; the alcalde could be appointed by a town council or higher authorities; he was the head of the civilian government in a city or larger political unit; an alcalde served as a judge in both civil and criminal cases

Canister: a type of artillery projectile that delivered many musket balls in a spreading pattern like a huge shotgun

Carronade: a stubby cannon designed to fire large projectiles of various types at short range; lighter than regular artillery, it could be operated by a much smaller crew at a higher rate of fire

Corvette: a fast handling sleek three masted ship smaller than a frigate, but larger than a brig or sloop; corvettes usually carried fewer than twenty cannon

Escudo: a gold Spanish coin worth sixteen ounces of silver

Gelding: a neutered male equine; geldings are gentler and easier to handle than stallions

Grape shot: an artillery projectile formed from stacked rows of large round shot of roughly one pound each; depending on the size of the gun firing the grape shot, it could be as few as nine or dozens; it was used at short to medium range against massed troops or light defenses; its range was greater than canister and far less than solid shot

Hogging: a serious structural defect of a wooden ship where the backbone or keel of the ship loses its strength through damage or decay; when this occurs the bow and stern sag away from the middle of the ship making it very difficult to maneuver and prone to sinking in even slightly rough seas

Labor: a Spanish unit of land measurement equal to 177 acres

League: a Spanish unit of land measurement equal to 4428 acres; also a distance of roughly 2.6 miles

Letter of marquee and reprisal: official government documents allowing a private warship to raid enemy ships; undocumented ships were considered pirates

Mordida: Spanish for "little bite"; a bribe, or less often, a tip for good service

Morral: a crudely made bag with carrying straps usually woven from grass, fiber or coarse cloth

Nacogdoches (nac ah doh' chez): an important settlement in eastern Texas the Camino Real which was the center of government for that part of Texas

Natchitoches (nac' ah tosh): an important center of trade at the junction of the Camino Real and the Red River in Louisiana; the Red River connected it with the Mississippi River and all points north and south on that vital waterway; an overland road connected it to Natchez, Mississippi on the banks of the Mississippi River where the famous Natchez Trace connected overland to the east

Pannier: canvas or leather cargo containers made to fit pack saddles

Piloncillo: brown sugar formed into a hard cone, often wrapped in paper

Powder hoy: a specially designed ship made to load gunpowder on to ships

Redoubt: a heavily fortified area in a line of defensive works, often projecting ahead of the line to protect vulnerable points

Scow: an oared boat used to travel against the current, especially in a river, sometimes assisted by a single lug sail

Soldado: a soldier

Sweet sorghum: also called ribbon cane; an annual crop used to produce syrup known as sorghum molasses; the juice was pressed out, then slowly heated to remove impurities and thicken to the desired consistency; in many part of the country, sugar was very expensive, so sorghum molasses was the common sweetener

# Suggested Reading

Campbell, Randolph B. Gone to Texas: a history of the Lone Star State. New York: Oxford University Press. 2003

Cantrell, Gregg. Stephen F. Austin, Empressario of Texas. New Haven: Yale University Press. 1999

LaVere, David. The Texas Indians. College Station, Texas: Texas A&M University Press. 2004

Meyers, Michael C.; Sherman, William L.; Deeds, Susan M. The Course of Mexican History, 7th Edition. New York: Oxford University Press. 2003

Miller, Robert R. Mexico: A History. Norman Oklahoma: University of Oklahoma Press. 1985

Newcomb, W.W., Jr. The Indians of Texas. Austin, Texas: University of Texas Press. 1999

Teja, Jesus F. de la. San Antonio de Bexar. Albuquerque, New Mexico: University of New Mexico Press. 1995